In Search of Heaven

In Search of Heaven

Ata Servati

To obtain more information about the writer, go to *www.sennapictures.com*

Library of Congress Number:		20044092893
ISBN:	Hardcover	0-9779747-0-7
	Softcover	0-9779747-1-5

This book was released in June 2006.
This book was printed and bound in the United States of America.

Special Thanks and Appreciation to:

Abbas Pahlevan, Mohammad Ehsani,
Andrew Ettinger, Kristy Servati,
Senna Servati, Farnaz Servati,
Roxanna Wiles, Sara Nejatroshan, Terry Porter,
Lezly Cavana, Kenny Saylors, Kyle Saylors,
Soufi Siadat, Anton Petach, Dr. Hassan Kalantary and all
of who, helped me with research
and other aspects of the book.
And my salute to Julie Benson
for her wonderful design and artwork
on the covers and inside of the book.
and special thanks to
Bradley Fischder who first inspired
me to turn this script into a book,

Ata Servati

I cry ...
I cry for the holy city of Tabriz,
The fabled home of the Garden of Eden
I cry for the breathless city of Orumieh,
Birthplace of Adam and Eve
Home of Zarathustra, who gifted us
Good words, Good thought, Good deeds.

I cry for the inspiring land of Shiraz,
Resting home of Cyrus the Great,
Home of Hafez, Saddi and Persepolis
I cry for the land of King Cyrus,
Creator of justice for our civilization,
Founder of the first declaration of human rights.

I cry for land of the lion, land of the sun,
Birthplace of civilization, farming and postal
I cry for Esphahan, known as paradise
Eyes may not believe what they see,
but the heart does.

I cry for the land of spirituality, land of colorless,
The ageless land of Khaghani, Rumi, Omar Khayyam
I cry for the land of poetry, science and love,
Ferdosi, Ebne Senna and Zakaria Razy
Few to call.

I cry for Persia, now called Iran

Invaded, plundered, raped and burned,
By bandits, barbarians and evildoers
But people's spirits always stand free and tall.

I cry for America's Howard Baskerville,
Son of Iranian freedom, as called by Sardar
I am no longer me, I am Persia
As Howard's final words were.

I cry for peace, I cry for love,
Between Christian, Muslim, Jew, Hindus
Zoroastrian, Buddhist and all men
As the Christ and all other holly messengers
wished for all.

Because,
We are all colorless as God looks up on us
We are all a passenger
Came from earth, breathe the same air
Going through uncertain life

And then
Will return back into the earth.
And become one
Regardless if we wish or not,
The choice is not ours
The final word is always goodbye.

Ata Servati

Foreword

In retrospect, this story was committed to paper fairly quickly. Actually, it took over thirty years to seriously convince myself that the time was right to finish its telling. My departure from my homeland in 1975 left me yearning for something special, something close to my heart that expressed my political beliefs. I delayed relating the story, a somewhat sad and murky tale, waiting for something, and it seems writing about it was just that something I was waiting for.

I was in preparation for a film project, "Dream on Empty," here in Los Angeles, when I was reunited with Abbas Pahlevan at a gathering at my home. It had been quite some time since I had last seen him. He was once the chief editor of the magazine *Ferdossi* in Iran. His periodical published an article about me in which I was compared to a Samad Behrangy, a well-known writer/activist who had drowned, in mysterious circumstances, in a river that flowed through the city of Tabriz, the setting of the story before you. I had heard that some of the staff had encountered problems because of the article. And I had avoided Abbas ever since. After all, very few people like going out of their way to get yelled at.

Ironically, he ended up becoming a neighbor of a lifelong friend of mine, Dr. Hassan Kalantary. Imagine my feelings when, after decades of dodging him, he showed up in my very living room. It was a busy gathering, and the house was full. But about two seconds after he saw and recognized me, he wanted to talk to me in private. Feeling that I was about to face some old music, I led him to my office. To my surprise, it was exactly the opposite of what I was expecting.

After I had made sure that he was without horns or fangs, we began conversing seriously. At some point in our conversation, I locked the door to the room. I was going to permit no interruptions from either my girlfriend or my guests until we had finished talking.

He related a truly interesting story about an American missionary named Howard Conklin Baskerville who, about a century ago, went to Iran and tried to reconcile the positive words of his Christian theology with the beliefs of the people there. It all sounded very interesting, enough to persuade me to set my current project aside and look into the story, despite the big financial loss involved.

I found that Howard had a powerful spiritual belief that united all people and transcended religious ideologies. He realized there is either a freedom that all people should share, that freedom being an inherent right to pursue and support righteous leadership in a democratic fashion according to their hearts' belief, or there is a spiritual dictatorship under which domineering and greedy men demand control because "it is God's will."

Howard managed, through word and deed, to inspire very downtrodden students to think, question and, ultimately, rebel against a terrible and repressive controlling faction that pretended to speak for God. It may sound like a simple story told often throughout history, but the political forces involved here are still very much in effect at the present time.

In 1908, Howard Baskerville realized that all movement toward positive social change had to come from the people. To this end, they had to first learn what was really going on in their country. He addressed the realities of the time, letting the people know that their only hope toward freedom of thought, belief, or deed was to realize that their king and clergy had sold out Iran to the interests of Great Britain and the czar of Russia.

To make a long story short, Howard had to tackle the difficult issue of morality versus reality. At the time, there was a secret plan by England and Russia to divide Iran into "Northern" and "Southern" districts, with the English controlling the south and Russians, the north.

By example, through his faith and awareness, Howard created hope among the people in Tabriz and brought them to rally around the national hero of Iran, Sattar Khan, and thereby frustrate the plans of these foreign interests.

I hope Howard's example will stand as an enduring lesson to young people today: It is through their educated efforts, not outside influences, that the oppressive voices of God expounded by the clergy will be finally silenced.

After a TV special about the "Discovery of the Garden of Eden" was aired, my belief became much stronger that it was fate that led Howard to arrive in Tabriz. After many years of in-depth inquiry, after examining numerous documents, biblical references, archeological findings, and various holy texts and sources, the producers of the show had finally concluded that all signs pointed toward the city of Tabriz being the actual Garden of Eden. Next to Tabriz is the city of Orumiyeh (Rezaiyeh, 1926-1980) which they concluded, was the home of Adam and Eve.

Some power beyond Howard's understanding had drawn him into the depths of Persian philosophy and metaphysics. He was amazed to learn that the roots of civilization lay in Persia, within the Zagros Mountains, where human beings had left the mountain and gathered in the valley. That was the beginning of farming and the domestication of animals, which eventually resulted in the creation of villages and then cities. In fact, like the Italians and the Germans, Persians are descended from the Aryans. And one can clearly see the influence of Persian philosophers in later German developments that changed the course of the history of philosophy.

Howard soon realized that the state of mind and the culture of Persians differed dramatically from those of Americans and Europeans. Their spirituality was apparent everywhere. Their most prized possessions were not material goods: they were each other and the land that gave them the resources to survive. Their generosity and understanding of humanity showed Howard and many others that our lives are all equally important.

Perhaps that was why Howard was fascinated and influenced by the philosophy of Cyrus the Great, king of Persia in the fifth century B.C. and author of the world's first declaration of human rights.

Cyrus spoke often about the importance of human rights. His method of governing was based on the ideal of justice for all. He followed a strict code in his dealings with all the countries that were subject to his rule. This was to create wealth, not plunder resources; to build rather than destroy; to permit freedom of speech; and to give people the chance to live in peace.

Howard would constantly remind his students and revolutionary friends of King Cyrus's philosophy of human rights. And to his students and others, he liked to read the text of the human rights charter issued by Cyrus the Great in 539 B.C. for the freedom of nations in Babylon:

"I am Cyrus, King of Kings, Great King, Powerful King, King of Babylon, King of Sumer and Akkad, King of four countries. Son of Kambujieh the Great King, King of Shahr Enshan, grandson of Cyrus the Great - King from the eternal dynasty whose descendants are covered by the affection of Ahura Mazda and whose government is close to the hearts of the people.

"When I entered Babylon with tranquility and friendship, I sat on the throne at the palace of Babylon Kings, amidst the joy and happiness of all the people. Marduk (the Chief Babylonian God), whose exaltation I always sought, turned the hearts of the noble people of Babylon towards me. My great army moved peacefully inside the city of Babylon. I let no harm come to the people of this city and the land of Sumer and Akkad. I ordered that all people were free to worship their own God and that atheists not harm them, that none of the houses of the people be destroyed and that nobody deprive the inhabitants of the city of the means of earning their livelihood, that all the Temples in the cities of Babylon, Ashu, Shush, Akkad, and in all the lands situated on the other side of Dejleh, erected in olden times and closed now, to be opened. I returned all the Gods of these Temples to their respective places, to be stationed there always. I also returned the Gods of Sumer and Akkad, brought by Nebonid to Babylon and causing anger in their Palace called 'Happiness of Heart.' All the kings living in all the countries of the world, from upper sea to lower sea, and the kings of the west who lived in tents, brought their precious gifts to Babylon and presented them to me."

In the land of Cyrus the Great, circa 1907, people faced the usual problems of government oppression, foreign invaders, the defiling of their beliefs, and the pillaging of their lands for resources, expansion or exploitation.

The principles of freedom, justice and tolerance that Howard and Sardar believed in, and fought so fiercely for, are under similar attack a century later. During their glory days, Howard, Sardar and other heroes rose in righteous rebellion against the injustices of not only two powerful external oppressors, the Russian and British empires, but also against the enemies of liberty within their own land.

Sadly, today the internal politics of the country have become an even more severely intricate dance of devils, death and destruction.

We must remember the heroic acts of Howard and his valiant companions. They did not fight to support an oppressive government or establish one religious belief in place of all others. Instead, they courageously laid down their lives in hopes that their countrymen would have the right to govern themselves and practice their religion as guided by God.

Although this particular struggle for freedom occurred in the Mideast a century ago, it's not that different from what's occurring in the present. Thus, it is my honor to dedicate this book to all the valiant young people of Iran who continue to strive for the good of their country, who continue to bravely work for peace and justice.

We must remember with respect and appreciation all of those worthy souls who have died, been jailed or have disappeared without a trace for this cause. I humbly bow to all of you, and pray for your well being.

May you join the ranks of kindred souls such as Amir Kabeer, Muhammed Mossadegh, Reza Shah Pahlavi I, Sattar Khan, Bagher Khan, Howard Baskerville and so many others who have challenged oppression and injustice in Iran, and may you triumph. It is time for the tolerance, amity and justice envisioned so long ago by Cyrus the Great to come to reality.

From all I hold dear, I thank all my readers. Please refer this book to others so that we may step toward peace and love in this world. I have added character descriptions at the end of the text to make it easier for those who are unfamiliar with Iranian names to follow the story.

Ata Servati

Chapter One

Realities Collide

Everything we love dies. Yet we go on pushing reality away while we grasp for moments of meaning to justify our lives.

New York City, 1949. The Iranian embassy has set up a conference to celebrate Persian literature.

Reza Zadeh Shafagh, a middle-aged Iranian man, is among the speakers at the conference. Reza has an exceptionally broad forehead and a receding hairline, with soft thin curls; this makes him look babyish and sweet. But Reza, who has come all the way from Persia, is feeling heavy-hearted.

A reflection in a shop window had reminded him of an old friend. Thoughts of the past come swimming back. Reza has come to talk about Saddi, a Persian poet and philosopher. He is scheduled to be the last speaker at the conference. But now he seems preoccupied with things far from the subject of the conference.

A hotel receptionist brings a note to his room. After she leaves, he opens the note and reads:

Dr. Reza Zadeh Shafagh (Hajji Agha)

Dear Dr. Reza,

I was happy to see your name amongst the list of conference speakers. For personal reasons, I cannot see you in person. I'm watching from a distance, and it gives me great pleasure and happiness. Oh, I must say you have changed very much, but it's of no matter. Because you were one of Howard's students and best friends, I respect you, and you will always remain dear to me. I will try to leave you more messages.

With great respect,
Helen

Reza rushes out in search of the receptionist. Unshod and breathless, he arrives in the lobby and finds her back at her desk.

"Who gave you this note? Would you please point her out to me? Is she still here?"

"Sir, there was no lady. It was a boy."

"A boy?"

"Yes, a young boy!" She looks around. "I think he's gone."

"A young boy? Would you please check a name for me? Is

there a Helen Wilson registered at this hotel?"

She begins to scan her ledger. Reza takes a handkerchief out of his pocket and wipes his forehead.

"I'm afraid not, sir. There is no Helen Wilson on our list. No one by that name."

He can feel the hot Tabriz sun on his cheeks. He is reminded of the old, white, crumbling wall of the Memorial School. His eyes are covered with dust and blood, and the feel of cold metal fills the palm of his hand. Old memories.

He goes back to his room and climbs into bed. Unexpectedly, he sleeps well.

The conference room is packed the next day. The conference has just got under way. A lecture is already in progress. Reza is among a group of other speakers at the conference. But his attention is divided: From time to time, he anxiously scans the crowd.

A young man comes up to him and hands him a note. "I apologize for interrupting you, sir. But this note is for you." He walks away. Reza reads the note:

Dear Dr. Reza,

It seems that I have troubled you. That was not my intention. It's just that you remind me of my dear Howard. There is a serious reason why I cannot meet with you, and I ask you not to seek me out, but I am watching you very closely. I trust your lecture will be well received. I will be at the conference tomorrow night to hear your speech.

I wish you only the best,
Helen

Reza hurries after the man who had given him the note, and

finally reaches him just before he leaves the room.

"Where is the boy who gave you this note? Show him to me!"

The man is taken aback by Reza's vehemence. "Actually, it was a young girl, the one who gave me the note. It wasn't a boy."

"Is she here? Can you point her out?"

The man looks around, "She's gone, sir. I can't see her. She's gone," and he leaves.

Reza looks around and then hurries out. He moves through the hotel lobby, reaches the street, looking for Helen.

Finally, the last day of the conference. Despite the disturbance of the previous two days, Reza has slept well, too well, in fact. He has overslept. After a hasty toilet and an even hastier breakfast, he hurries into the conference room. It is the last day.

"Are you ready? You are next," the harassed-looking conference organizer asks. But Reza, distractedly scanning the room, seems not to hear.

This throws the man into a panic. He grabs Reza's shirt sleeve. "Dr. Reza, are you okay? You're next."

Reza looks through him: "I cannot talk about Saddi."

A brief, tense silence ensues.

Reza continues, "I have a new subject to talk about."

Meanwhile, Reza's introduction is being given: "And the final lecture of this conference belongs to Dr. Reza Zadeh Shafagh. He will speak about Saddi, the Iranian poet and philosopher. Ladies and gentlemen, Dr. Reza Zadeh Shafagh!"

The room applauds as Reza climbs the steps to the speaker's dais. For a few moments, he says nothing. He searches the crowd for the familiar, never-forgotten face.

Then, finally, Reza begins: "My friends, I know all of you are here to learn about Saddi. But a set of recent events has made me rethink things. I feel that if I do not first share this with you, I may do an injustice to a great man. This may well be the only opportunity I have to express my country's gratitude to an extraordinary human being. A man who came from a small town in Nebraska..." Tears appear in Reza's eyes, and his voice cracks, "A man called..."

* * *

On a small farm in Nebraska, a family has gathered to celebrate the graduation of their son from Princeton University. The year is 1907, the month May, and the young man's name is Howard Conklin Baskerville.

Howard Conklin Baskerville

Howard is slightly under six feet tall. His looks are pleasing. He has a mop of thick brown hair, bushy eyebrows and beautiful, full-color eyes.

Just four years earlier he had left the United States Army, after accidentally shooting and killing a horse in a training exercise. As he was staring at the dead horse, everything was frozen for him. Lost in thought, he could not even hear his drill sergeant yelling at the top of his voice. "What," Howard wondered, "if I kill a man one day? I cannot handle seeing even a dead horse." Then he recalled his pastor's voice. "Jesus came to teach us to love one another, not to hate; to help one another, not to hurt; to heal one another, not to kill."

Later that day Howard sat in a church, quietly staring at a statue of Christ. The voice of his drill sergeant was sharp in the stillness.

"This is why you choose to quit? You would rather pray for your country to be safe than fight for it? You are one of the best soldiers I have ever seen. You will rise high in no time, son. You were born a soldier."

"If that is true, Sergeant, then I am a soldier of peace, not war. 'Thou shall not kill . . .'"

"You are giving up the chance to do something good for yourself and your nation. You have the opportunity to travel all around the word with your unit and see and experience other nations and cultures. Don't throw away your future because of an accident."

It was then that Howard suddenly realizes that his heart's desire lay in peace. He wants to help people, not kill them. But not just his own people. He realizes his drill sergeant is right, that he was born a soldier. But he was born as a soldier of God. He would become a missionary and help others. And so Howard enters Princeton University to study history so he could understand and help others.

He has chosen Princeton for its program that found positions for students in missionary work after graduation. He had recently applied to work as a missionary. A few days before his graduation, he was offered a post at the Presbyterian Mission's

Memorial School in Tabriz in Persia, present-day Iran.

Persia, let alone Tabriz, had not been Howard's first choice. But it was far away and Howard was pleased by the prospect of doing good in such a remote place. He knew little about Persia. It had only exotic associations for him, picked up from romantic literature: beautiful and complaisant dark-haired women with long, lush raven-black hair; ruined castles; thirteen centuries of culture and architecture; mountains and an antique sea. It was something to look forward to. And he did.

* * *

Howard is being lifted upward, toward a darkening sky, by two angels, each wearing a long silk robe, one of green, one of blue. The angels float through rosy clouds that vanish abruptly. Howard sees shimmering multicolored spheres of light, which flow into rainbow tunnels of light. He and the angels pass through the tunnels and arrive in a pristine, ethereal garden filled with fruit and nut trees of every kind and all varieties of flowers in bloom. Mountains surround the garden; there is a four-branched river. They land on a riverbank. Howard looks around and then asks "What is this place?"

The angel in green answers, "The Garden of Eden."

Howard is surprised. "The Garden of Eden? How did you find it?"

The angel in blue says, "We didn't. You did."

Howard sees a man walking in the distance, looking much like Christ's image from the cross. As the figure drifts out of sight, Howard turns to the angels. "Did I just see Jesus?"

The angels smile but do not respond.

Howard looks back into the garden. He sees an unfamiliar man puttering about. "Who is that man?"

The angel in green replies, "Your friend. That is why you are here. You have come to visit him." "My friend?" Howard looks at the man, who smiles at him but walks away.

Howard's curiosity is aroused. He follows the mysterious man. Howard extends his arms like wings. Bright streaks of colored lightning flash toward him like weapons, but none strikes his body. Inspired, Howard runs after the man . . .

Howard is awakened from his dream by his two sisters, who are giggling.

* * *

The family has come to see Howard off at the station. He will travel across the country and then across an ocean to Persia. He sees the tears appears on his little sister's eyes. He is very close to them. They are all sad for him to leave but he is excited.

"Howard," his mother says softly, "You have just graduated with a degree in history from Princeton University. Your whole life is ahead of you."

Chapter Two

From the Middle West to the Middle East

Howard leans out of the cramped carriage. A warm breeze plays on his face. The year is 1908, and he is about to cross the Ghafgha's border of Iran. Something in this alien heat, this alien sun, warms him to the core. He is bursting with excitement.

The carriage driver announces the approach of the checkpoint. Howard is momentarily blinded by the sun. He can barely make out the border or the earth-colored buildings scattered throughout the surrounding landscape. Dust rises from the solid ground as the carriage comes to a stop at the checkpoint.

When the dust clears, Howard is surprised to see a number of rough soldiers standing guard with rifles dangling from their shoulders. They approach the carriage, and the driver gets out quickly, papers in hand.

One of the soldiers, possibly an officer, looks over the papers; there is an expression of watchfulness on his face. The soldier isn't what Howard was expecting. He looks foreign. Could he be Russian? He is. The Russian finishes examining the papers. When he looks up, he meets Howard's gaze. They stare at each other, which leads to an uncomfortable silence within the carriage.

Somehow, Howard finds the words.

"Howard Baskerville," he says, "from America."

The man's expression softens. He looks uncertain for just an instant.

"America?" he says softly, and hands the papers back to the carriage driver. He backs away, keeping a steady eye on Howard. Then he signals the soldiers to let the carriage pass through.

Howard begins to relax when the driver announces they will soon cross the natural border of Iran. Howard now becomes tense with every passing moment. A few minutes later, the carriage pulls up at the Iranian border. There is a large detachment of Russian soldiers at this border as well. And, once again, Howard catches their attention immediately.

The carriage driver goes through the same routine; he seems to know it well. He hands the passengers' papers to the officer in charge and waits quietly for directions. Several soldiers begin to unload and check the bags; others search the carriage and look the passengers up and down.

"They are mostly foreigners," the carriage driver says. "I checked their bags. They aren't carrying guns."

The officer regards the driver steadily. Finally, satisfied, he gives the order to let them pass. Five minutes later they are racing down the rough road, in a flurry of dust.

A little calmer now, Howard lets his eye travel over the countryside. A white horse, followed by a colt, catches his eye. They are moving very fast, about five hundred yards, Howard guesses, from the Russian border. They seem to be racing away from the border. They are unsaddled and move with an intensity and freedom that Howard has never seen before. He is riveted by the sight. He has never seen anything like it in his life.

His window glows reddish in the light of the setting sun as the carriage enters Baku. He is about to set foot in Iran for the first time. Worn out as he is, the prospect fills him with excitement.

His first impressions are hugely disappointing. He had been expected those grand castles and ravishing beauties with thick black hair. Persia, he had read, was heaven on earth.

This village did not fit that description. Where, he wonders, is the grandeur? And why are the women covered from head to toe in black sheets? He sees only mud houses and general poverty.

Howard looks around the village. Big brown eyes stare at him through slits in the women's veils. He feels tired, stupid and disoriented.

He walks toward a small shop. He leans against a wall, cooling off in the shade. The walls of these mud houses, he notices, are two yards thick; the windows and doors are all wooden. Colorful pieces of cloth cover the floors and chairs; there are beautiful handmade rugs on the floor.

The wild white horse and her colt catch his eye again. They are in the village now, and putting on a show. Young men surround the wild creatures; perhaps, Howard thinks, they are trying to catch the horses.

The sound of a drum echoes through the village. Howard looks up. The drummer is a blind young chubby-faced boy, sitting on the rooftop of an old, run-down house.

The carriage driver approaches. "It is a song of war," he tells Howard. "He is playing a religious war song."

A crowd has gathered to watch the young men and the horses.

A competition of some kind is in progress. The young men are loud, challenging one another. The horses seem to be toying with them. When, unaccountably, a horse passes near him, Howard, overcome by the spirit of the moment, lunges for the horse, only to miss. The crowd cheers him on. Howard is extremely embarrassed.

A boy, probably no more than fifteen, grabs the white mare boldly with both hands and jumps on her back. He moves with the movement of the horse's body. He stays on, as the wind sweeps through his hair.

The crowd has grown by now, and all eyes are on the boy. Howard smiles enviously at the beauty and skill of the youth.

The cheering dies down all of a sudden. A uniformed Russian has been spotted riding toward them from the direction of the border. He is followed by another soldier. The crowd scatters and the drumming comes to an abrupt stop.

Howard looks up at the blind drummer, wondering how he knew. He could see the fear in his solemn expression, in the way he sat perfectly still, waiting for the worst. It was as if he could smell danger pounding its way across the dirt and the dust.

Several men yell nervously at the other boy to get off the horse. But he won't listen. The villagers' reaction puzzles and disturbs Howard. He cannot understand their nervousness. Or is it fear? A knot develops in his stomach. He stands perfectly still, not knowing what to do. The blind boy gets up slowly and begins to pound his drum deliberately, one note after another. It is as if he were matching the rhythmic pounding of the Russian horses' hooves.

The Russian in the lead, an officer, Howard realizes, reaches the village and rides straight up at full speed to the boy astride the horse. As the boy circles him, a whip made of thick brown leather appears at the side of the officer's horse. He takes a cut, then another; soon, the officer is whipping the boy with such force that lines of dripping blood appear all over his body. A sadistic smile begins to form on the officer's face.

A crowd gathers. People watch helplessly. Howard sees contempt and anger on their faces; some cry, others just wait silently for it to end. Howard's feet are cemented to the ground. He can hardly breathe.

But the Russian has underestimated the strength of the boy. He is determined to stay on the horse. He holds on with all his might. Blood drips into his eyes and pours down the mane of the horse. It cannot last. Finally, the young boy loses his balance and falls. The beating continues as the boy lies on the ground, not moving an inch. The officer curses and screams at the crowd.

The other Russian soldier, who has been a passive spectator, retrieves the horse and rides back toward the crowd. The colt follows at a distance, hesitantly. The blind boy begins to sing, a deep cry more than a melody. His drum music is filled with fury and with every effort he stands up and sings toward the heavens.

Howard turns to the boy lying on the ground and notices a new look of determination in his eyes. As the beat of the drum intensifies, the boy begins to move slowly, as if gaining energy from the drummer's voice. He presses his hands into the dirt, and curls them up slowly; dirt fills a bloody palm. All of a sudden, the whip-wielding Russian is blinded by a fistful of dirt. As he flails his whip about, his bloody victim gets to his feet.

The boy is filled with strength and begins chanting to the beat of the drums, challenging the officer to get off his horse and fight like a man.

The Russian corners the boy, lashing out at each chance he gets. The villagers begin to close in on the two. The blind boy begins to shake and play ferociously and the people become angrier. As the drum gets louder, so do the cries of the people. They raise their fists and call to the heavens for help. Now, the injured boy can no longer see the whip as it swings through the air at him. As the sun reflects off the whip and lights it up for a moment, the boy is able to grab the reins of the Russian's horse. The officer tries to keep his balance but he off his horse, his right foot caught in the stirrup. The boy leans over and pulls the officer's foot out of the stirrup, and the officer tumbles to the ground. The boy stands over him, glaring into his eyes.

Howard's fists begin to ball up; he is enraged and fearful but wants, overwhelmingly, to do something. He moves forward, but the carriage driver quickly grabs his arm tightly and pulls him back. For a moment, there is complete silence except for the blind boy and his drum. Howard moves again and is stopped by the carriage driver once more. This time, however, he catches the officer's attention. They stare at each other for a moment. The Russian unholsters his gun, swings around on the ground, and shoots the boy madly, without taking his eyes off Howard. A smirk begins to forms on his face.

The officer rises to his feet and beckons to his companion to fetch his horse. He looks around the village contemptuously. Howard makes another movement but is again restrained by the driver.

A friend of the dead boy steps forward and throws a stick at the officer's head. The tears run down his face. He stands there, not moving an inch, as the officer withdraws his gun and, with careful deliberation, shoots him in the head. He falls slowly to the ground; the drum beats on. The Russian places his revolver back into its holster and then, as if for the first time, becomes aware of the drum. He looks up at the blind drummer.

The villagers, maddened beyond endurance, surround the officer. They give him no chance to pull out his gun. He disappears under a pile of angry men and women. The blind boy plays harder. And Howard feels his heart beat to the rhythm of the drum. He looks up and notices that the blind boy seems to be looking directly at him; he can feel the boy looking into his soul.

The other Russian gallops off toward the border, and a large group of villagers set off in pursuit. He lets go of the white horse and, holding his gun high in the air, fires a shot, which is a warning to his pursuers and a signal to the Russians across the border that help is needed. He disappears into the distance and the villagers abandon the chase.

The carriage driver herds his passengers into the carriage immediately. Howard raptly watches the blind drummer boy. The driver grabs Howard and shoves him in.

The sound of a third gunshot pulsates through Howard's ears. He turns and looks out the window to see the people slowly walking away from the dead Russian officer. A young boy stands over the dead officer, holding the gun firmly in his hand. Several older men and women yell at him to drop the gun and run. They scream over and over again. One man walks up and slaps him hard against his cheek, trying to grab the gun from the boy's firm grip, but he doesn't move.

The pounding of horses' hooves is heard. A large group of Russian soldiers, four hundred of them, are making their way across the border, heading straight for the village. The villagers scatter in panic. The soldiers shoot at anything that moves. Cats, dogs, cows, sheep, and humans begin to fall to the ground.

Howard can still hear the boy playing on the rooftop. As the Russians get closer, the drum beats louder and louder. Howard's eyes are fixed on the blind drummer. He is immobilized. He somehow feels he is no longer within his own body.

The carriage jolts up the rocky road, almost tipping over in the driver's haste. Howard, who is leaning out, is thrown from his seat and finds himself hanging onto the open door; his feet dangle inches from the ground. He holds on until the carriage stops. When they reach the top of a nearby hill, the driver stops and lets the passengers get out. Almost against their will they watch the bloody scene below them.

The boy with the gun runs toward the Russian soldiers, shooting frantically; the beat of the drum grows in intensity. Within seconds, the boy is riddled with bullets. Gun in hand, he sinks to his knees. The blind drummer stands up, beating out his death song with every fiber of his being. He looks up toward the hill, and Howard can feel his unseeing eyes boring into his skin.

His whole body begins to shake. The drummer boy suddenly tumbles to the ground with a bullet to the heart. His drum is still on the rooftop. Irritated, a soldier aims and shoots, filling it with a dozen bullet holes. It begins to roll down the roof and lands beside the blind boy's motionless hands. The soldier rides up and fires three more shots into the drum.

The music is replaced by sounds of gunfire and screaming; people everywhere are dropping to the ground.

Howard can barely grasp what he is seeing. Every standing structure in the village has been set ablaze. Smoke fills the air. Within minutes, all life within the village has ceased to exist. The Russians shoot even the chickens that are scampering about.

Howard turns to the driver of the carriage; tears are running down the man's cheeks. Everyone boards the carriage. Howard is dazed, inert. The driver tugs at his arm gently. He tells Howard softly that they have to leave. They set off in silence.

Howard is looking numbly out of the window when he sees a white horse moving fast in the same direction as the carriage. He wonders if he has made a mistake in coming to this country. But his faith steadies him. He tells himself that he is here for a reason that is, for the present, hidden from him.

It is now late in the afternoon, and the carriage is approaching the outskirts of Tabriz. As the carriage ascends a hill, the travelers see Tabriz is in the distance; they are only a few hours from their destination.

* * *

It is a cool and windy afternoon in the fall of 1908 as Howard rides into the ancient city of Tabriz for the first time. His gaze is fixed on the street.

The dirt road widens, and houses and people begin to appear. The women are covered from head to toe in colorful fabrics. Yellows, reds, blues, greens, and turquoise create intricate patterns of all kinds. A strange and beautiful sight! The shops look like giant adobe structures built out of handmade bricks. The bricks look old and weathered. The tallest buildings are but two stories high. Each store offers a different item: fresh bread, rugs, pottery, fresh vegetables; Howard sees a butcher shop.

On each side of the street, a small ditch separates the sidewalk from the dirt road. Trees line the street on both sides. Horses and carriages share the dirt road. The accumulated tension of the past hours is beginning to wane. The people of Tabriz seem friendly and welcoming; they have ready smiles and wave at the carriage.

A couple of young boys run alongside. The carriage stops, and the driver gets out and hands Howard his dusty red suitcase; he wishes him good luck and heads off down the winding road. Howard walks through the gate of the carriage station. He notices a small, scruffy dog tied to a pole and barking at every passing traveler. Howard smiles; he is suddenly reminded of home.

Everyone seems to be in a hurry and Howard can barely get anyone's attention. He speaks no Farsi, and he can't find anyone who looks American. He moves towards an old man who is resting against a wall. Howard says a few words in English. The man looks at Howard as if he's crazy. Howard mimes words and actions desperately. After a few moments, a crowd begins to gather.

Howard's discomfort becomes frustrating. He senses that people want to help but simply don't know what he wants. He repeats the words "Mission School" over and over again, to no effect.

Suddenly, a voice shouts out, "Memorial School, Memorial School!"

The voice belongs to a young boy in the back of the crowd.

"Yes! I am looking for the Memorial School," Howard says. "Do you know where it is?"

The boy nods and takes off down the street, beckoning Howard to follow. Howard grabs his suitcase and, after waving goodbye to the gathered crowd, follows the boy. He has trouble; his guide is keeping a steady pace, looking back occasionally to make sure Howard is still behind him. Howard wonders why they are running. His suitcase feels heavier and heavier. The boy stops, turns around, and runs toward Howard. He is relieved, thinking that now they will finally slow down and, perhaps, even walk. But the boy grabs the suitcase and places it on his head. He gives Howard a smile, turns around and begins to run again, motioning Howard to try to keep up. They run through several narrow alleys. Howard is amazed that the boy can run for so long with a suitcase on his head.

They finally reach an alley that leads to a wide, open street. The unknown boy stops in front of a large, old wooden door. A sign on the door says "Memorial School." Howard can see no building, just a tall, thick dirt wall. The boy sets the suitcase down, waves goodbye, and departs abruptly.

Howard, now more tired and bewildered than he has ever been, bends down to pick up his suitcase. Gunshots sound in the distance. He pushes open the door and enters.

Memorial School Building

The school building is before him, a tall brown-and-beige affair. The sun is beginning to set behind the mountains. The building goes pink in the dusky light.

Flanking the school are several residential buildings and, a bit farther away, a small church.

The dying light is in his tired eyes. Just then, he sees a woman carrying a bucket and walking toward a well. She has deep brown hair, with round soothing eyes. She is slender and walks with a certain grace.

Helen Wilson - 1908

Howard thinks she is the most beautiful woman he has ever seen. Sensing Howard's gaze, she looks up. They exchange a long, lingering look.

Howard's manners eventually assert themselves. He sets his suitcase down and smiles.

A man's voice breaks the deeply suggestive silence. "Ah! You must be the new teacher. Welcome, welcome!"

Howard looks up and sees a man of average height, with a strong but warm face and a salt-and-pepper bow-tie mustache.

Samuel Graham Wilson - 1907

"I am, yes," he says, and striding forward, holding out his hand. "Howard Baskerville."

"Samuel Wilson, headmaster. And this is my daughter, Helen."

Hands are shaken all round.

"You probably want to see your new home," Mr. Wilson says. "Good heavens, you've come a long way! You must be exhausted."

Howard is shown to one of the small cottages near the Presbyterian Memorial School building.

Howard is tired and would like nothing more than to rest, but something makes him want to prolong the scene.

"What is it like here?" he asks the headmaster.

Mr. Wilson explains, "It is very different from the States, but not worse or better in any particular way. We hardly go out and really become one with the locals, though. We have our own little community here and stay together. But the people are respectful, gracious, and full of energy; the land, well, you can see for yourself, it's stunning."

"Are you all right?" Mr. Wilson blocks the sun with his hand, trying to get a good look at Howard's face. Howard, who had lost himself in dreamy contemplation of the ravishing mountain scenery before him, turns towards Mr. Wilson. "Yes," he says. "Yes. I'm fine. Just tired. It's been a very long day."

Howard's cottage has a tiny kitchen, a bathroom, and a fairly large room containing a wooden bed and a beautiful, many-colored handmade rug that covers most of the floor.

Gunshots ring out nearby.

"It's quite different from the States here." Mr. Wilson is silent for a bit, nervous and uncomfortable. "I wonder what you make of what you've seen so far. I am sure you will find your way, with God's help. But now you must rest. Please join my family for dinner. I insist."

Howard smiles his acceptance, and the Wilsons leave.

He watches Helen walk across the yard to her house, a much larger cottage than his. Her father carries her bucket. Howard is happy that she lives so near. He sees the sun disappearing behind the mountain.

* * *

Howard makes his way through the darkness to the Wilsons' house. Mr. Wilson greets him at the door and takes him inside. After all the introductions are made, he retires to his favorite chair and lights his pipe.

Helen's mother, Annie Rhea Wilson, is tall and plain looking. She seems both kind and intelligent. Not the beauty that Helen is, but Howard thinks there is something of her in Helen. Susan, Helen's younger sister, is busy in the kitchen. She is reserved, even, perhaps, a little nervous.

They talk about Iran. Howard is surprised to learn that Mrs. Wilson was born in Orumiyeh in northwest Iran. Her father was a minister named Samuel Rhea who served as a missionary. Her parents arrived in April of 1860 and stayed until her father's death in 1865. Annie returned to America with her mother and three siblings: Robert, Foster, and Sophia. After completing her education she married the Reverend Samuel Wilson. Soon afterward, she found herself back in the same country she had loved as a child, with her very own family.

Four candles are placed on the table; Annie grabs a fifth one and sets it on the table as well. Each candle represents a member of the family. The fifth is for Howard. He is grateful for his welcome. A colorful centerpiece of wildflowers has been placed in the middle of the table and fills the room with a fresh fragrance. It mixes with the aroma from the kitchen and makes Howard yearn for both food and sleep.

They all take their seats and join hands as Mr. Wilson rises to say grace. They follow with closed eyes. Everyone quietly mumbles "amen" and they raise their heads. Helen is the talker in the family. She wants to get Howard talking but doesn't want to seem pushy.

"Father enjoys short prayers and long dinners," she says. "How about you, Howard?"

Howard smiles. "Both activities are necessary and satisfying, Helen."

Howard is curious about the reserved Susan. But Mr. Wilson, who has been away from the States for a long time, is eager for news.

Howard swallows. "Well, as always, the papers are still setting the standards and policies. No one goes a day without reading one now; they make the nation tick. The men work hard in the fields, unless they live in the city, and have too many drinks when they are done. Then they fight. The women care for the children and hold their families and households together."

The conversation lasts through dinner and continues in the living room; Mr. Wilson smokes his pipe and listens, his eyes half closed.

They all genuinely like Howard and enjoy listening to him. Susan alone is sleepy and uninterested.

But Helen warms to her subject. "It's interesting how a society which dedicates itself to being of service to so many helpless nations seems to fall apart within its own foundation."

Howard looks at Helen admiringly. "Yes," he says, "America has its problems, I will give you that, but there's no other place that gives one the same opportunities to be true to oneself."

Mr. Wilson opens his eyes, "That is true; but as with any sort of freedom, you must sacrifice something else for it. But, yes, you make a very good point."

It is late. Howard excuses himself, thanking them for their hospitality and the conversation. Helen's eyes never leave Howard. Annie notices and smiles to herself.

Helen is restlessly awake that night. Her thoughts are full of Howard and sleep comes with difficulty. She has a dream. She and Howard are married and living in the States. They have a farmhouse with several children running around. They seem blissfully happy. She wakes up the next morning, disappointed by drab reality.

* * *

Howard is taken to see the sights by Helen. They are in a carriage owned by the Memorial School. Howard is struck by the way the men greet one another. They remove their hats and bow, one hand across their heart. Helen explains that this is a Persian custom. In Persia, you always respect your elders, whatever their social condition. How right that is, Howard thinks. He feels a sudden surge of warmth for the place.

The carriage stops in front of Tabriz's biggest bazaar, and they enter. The bazaar is the center of local commerce; all goods are distributed there. There are two kinds of shops within the city; those that sell to the public at retail, and wholesalers. Each bazaar is filled with hundreds of shops, all carrying the same merchandise. Gold, silver, and fine gemstones are the main commodities. The people who control the bazaar are very powerful. Their influence is felt in every aspect of local life; for instance, they even control religious leaders. It is, as always, a question of money. The government watches them very closely.

Howard is fascinated by the amount of gold and silver in the shops and the ornate architecture. Every corner of the place is decorative. Some shops are hundreds of years old.

Bazaar in Tabriz

Howard finds himself revived with feelings of great warmth. This is unexpected and very gratifying. During the course of the day, he learns also that one has to be able to bargain. If one were adept, one could get almost anything at a good price.

They have just left the bazaar when they see a Russian carriage speed down the street; it is escorted by several mounted Russians. Just then, a little boy runs out into the street.

Howard and Helen watch as the little boy is run over. The

carriage and the escort continue at full speed. Howard pulls Helen into a corner quickly and blocks her line of vision with his body. He doesn't want her to see the dead boy. People rush to the scene. A large crowd quickly gathers around the boy.

They walk to the school carriage. The driver, Abbass, is waiting. "If it wasn't for my family, I would grab a gun and shoot the bastards. In fact, if I were truly a man I would have already done it." Helen takes Howard by the arm and they board the carriage quietly. Howard stares helplessly at Abbass all the way home. He wants to say or do something for him, but what? What could he possibly do?

* * *

A Sunday morning. Howard has been in Tabriz for a few days now and has been kept very busy. But today the school is closed. People are beginning to make their way to church in the school compound. Most of the Americans and some wealthy local people are usually in attendance. It is a small church, seating about two hundred people, but decorated beautifully.

Howard accompanies the Wilsons. Helen has taken on the job of introducing Howard to everyone. Her beauty has made her popular among people. But it has her kindness that everyone remembers most. Helen has been much happier since Howard's arrival. On their way to church, she introduces him to several other families. A few young women are immediately interested in the handsome young teacher, but Helen maneuvers herself between them.

A women's choir is singing. The small church is full. Howard sits beside Helen in a pew separate from the other Wilsons.

Howard had marked this seat from the moment he walked in. It was the first aisle to the right, second row from the front.

The minister, Dr. Vanneman, stands in front of the choir, ready to give his Sunday sermon. Above his head and to his right is a statue of Christ.

Howard's gaze is fixed on the statue. He stares deep into its eyes. He is overwhelmed by the feeling that Christ is watching him. Helen whispers into his ear but he is deaf to her. He attracts the attention of a couple of people. He tries to rise from his seat. Helen grabs him and holds him down. His behavior is attracting attention.

He turns to Helen, who is very concerned by now, and says quietly, "I'm all right. I really am."

The pastor's sermon is about Tabriz and the necessity for patience, unity, and faith in Christ.

Howard has excited everyone's interest. Sincere, handsome, and intelligent, he is an obviously charismatic young man. The young women's eyes are on him. But his eyes are on the floor.

Outside, afterward, people approach Howard and introduce themselves. Howard is affability itself.

* * *

The sun shines more brightly even than usual in Tabriz. In one classroom of the Memorial School there is more than the usual uproar among students. Today their new American teacher is to appear before them for the first time and noisy speculation about him is under way. Howard's students are from the wealthiest and best-educated families of Tabriz. Among them are Reza Zadeh-

Shafagh (aka Hajji Agha), who is of average size, the somewhat large Hussein Khan, and the slightly rotund Mohtamedol Tojjar, who always dresses as if he were on his way to a party. There are many others, but these three command the most interest and attention.

The door opens and Mr. Wilson enters, followed by Howard. There is silence. The students look at Howard and then at each other. He is not fat, not bald, and not old!

Mr. Wilson takes off his glasses and wipes them. "If you gentlemen would spare me a moment. This is your new history teacher, Mr. Howard Baskerville. I'm sure he is as impressed by your manners as I am." He gives Howard a parting smile, "All yours, Mr. Baskerville."

But Howard is staring at a chubby-faced boy sitting all the way in the back of the class. He looks identical to the blind drummer boy in the massacred village. But that boy was shot dead! The whole class stares at Howard as he walks to the back of the room.

He whispers to the drummer's "twin," "Do you have a brother?"

Silence. Howard gazes blankly across the room.

"No, sir," Hajji Agha's voice breaks the silence. "He is deaf, sir. He is new. He came just a few weeks ago."

Howard turns back to the deaf boy. "Do you play the drums?" he asks. Then he remembers and seeks out Hajji Agha.

"Yes, he does, sir. A religious kind of drum called tabl." Hajji Agha sounds surprised. "When was the last time he played his drum?"

"Sir, that drum is used only once a year, for a special religious ceremony. The last one was four months ago. So, he played his drum exactly four months ago, sir."

The whole class is now completely mystified. Howard has known all along that his student could not be the blind drummer at the village. And yet, and yet! And he was deaf! And the resemblance was astonishing.

All the students stare at their new teacher in surprised silence. Howard looks around the room. He walks to the back of the class and back up to the front. Then he turns to them and says, "You do have beautiful manners! May I ask why you are so silent?"

Hajji Agha speaks for the whole class. "We did not expect you to be so young, sir."

Howard laughs and laughs. The students watch him with uncertainly. Then they join him in wholehearted laughter. Howard has won them over effortlessly. They all genuinely begin to like Howard. This is the best, the shortest-seeming class they have had in a long time. The time simply flies. When the bell rings, they leave reluctantly.

Howard soon follows Mr. Wilson into the break room where the teachers gather between classes. The room is full of both Iranians and Americans. To Howard, it seems very relaxed.

An Iranian in his late thirties, a man of more than ordinary dignity, with something commanding about him, rises to his feet. This is a gesture of respect to the new teacher. The others, perhaps reluctantly, follow his lead.

Mr. Wilson performs the introductions. The Iranian takes the lead in shaking Howard's hand as well. He is smiling, warm, welcoming. His name is Muhammed Hassan Sharifzadeh and he teaches philosophy at the school.

Howard is greatly taken with him. The difference between Mr. Sharifzadeh and the others is overwhelmingly obvious. In addition to everything else that sets him apart, Mr. Sharifzadeh dresses differently: He wears a turban around his head and a long robe is draped across his shoulders.

Mohammad Hassan Sharifzadeh

No one sits until Mr. Sharifzadeh sits. And Mr. Sharifzadeh will not sit until Howard does. Finally, Mr. Sharifzadeh points to a chair and motions Howard to sit down.

Howard soon learns that in Persia, on the arrival of someone older, everyone younger gets to his feet and waits until the older party is seated. But when an older, or widely respected, person does the same for someone younger, it demonstrates the modesty of the elder and does extraordinary homage to the younger.

There is a plate of Persian pastries and fruit on a table. A school helper brings a tray full of tea and cups, and offers them first to Mr. Sharifzadeh, who is sitting nearest the door. Mr. Sharifzadeh asks that Howard be served first.

"It would not be good manners to drink before our new friend," he says in his regal way.

Unused to such courtliness, Howard is momentarily at a loss. And he doesn't drink tea. He thanks the helper, fumbles with his cup, and takes a sip. Mr. Sharifzadeh hands cups of tea to two other teachers before taking one for himself. Howard watches closely as Mr. Sharifzadeh places a sugar cube in his mouth, then takes a sip of the tea slowly; everyone else does the same. One or two sips are enough to dissolve the sugar cube. Then they put another one in their mouths. It's interesting for Howard to experience their tea break.

An American teacher, Mr. John N. Wright, introduces himself to Howard. He demonstrates the Iranian tea ritual for Howard. Howard follows suit.

Mr. Sharifzadeh has been following all this. He smiles. He, too, is taken with Howard, indeed, likes him immediately.

Mr. Sharifzadeh intrigues Howard, who wonders how this Muslim clergyman has come to teach at a Christian school.

He wants very much to get to know him. Mr. Wilson's entrance interrupts Howard's thoughts. Everyone rises. Many conversations get under way. People offer helpful suggestions for Howard. Mr. Sharifzadeh himself volunteers any assistance that Howard might need.

* * *

The Americans in the compound are a small, self-contained group. They seldom go among the local people. They leave the compound and go into the city only when there is a pressing need. Howard, on the other hand, spends all his free time in the city among the people, asking questions and having conversations. He is extremely curious about this new world in which he has found himself. His openness and friendliness quickly make him a favorite among the locals.

* * *

Howard begins to settle in. His students like him very much. The relationship between the students and their teacher has deepened. Howard is their teacher but also their friend. Sometimes he is even more friend than teacher. For that time and place, this is extremely unusual. His students are doing well; hardly anyone ever misses a class. Howard is close to all his students, but he has become particularly close to Hajji Agha.

One afternoon, Hajji Agha arrives at Howard's doorstep, bearing hot Iranian bread. Howard is suspicious at first. He thinks Hajji Agha is currying favor. But Hajji Agha is a very good student, one of his best. So Howard sets aside his fears and settles down to his treat. They smear butter and honey on the bread, and it drips all over their hands. The outside is toasty and the inside is soft and fleshy.

Howard learnes to love hot bread and tea. From that day on, he wants fresh hot bread with every meal. Hajji Agha becomes Howard's official translator. He accompanies Howard everywhere and helps him acquire the rudiments of Farsi. They become close friends.

Helen teases Hajji Agha about his friendship with Howard, and says that she is jealous of him. There are occasions when she needs Hajji Agha's help to influence Howard on one matter or another. A friendship develops between Helen and Hajji Agha as well.

* * *

Tabriz, at this time, is full of uncertainty. The people are at the mercy of every stray rumor. Shopkeepers lock their doors without notice. The Kurds, led by a particularly ruthless man, are said to be marching towards Tabriz. They had lain waste to many villages in their path. Even worse news came. The Turks had entered Iran from the northwest and are approaching Tabriz. The mood in the city is one of panic.

Howard learns all this, and much more, every day, from Hajji Agha.

He takes Hajji Agha's hand and says, "God is with His people, and you will be okay. You are good people. God is with you." In the beginning, Hajji Agha was Howard's source of information. Later on, when he would learn more from Mr. Sharifzadeh, Howard would pass his information along to Hajji Agha.

One thing has become very clear to Howard: The shah's government is extremely corrupt.

The shah is incompetent and dishonest. His country is rapidly becoming the plaything of foreign powers: the English, the Russians, and the Turks. There is an acute danger of many Iranian border cities falling into Russian and Turkish hands. The shah, under the influence of the czar of Russia, is using Russian soldiers to suppress the uprisings that are spreading all over the country.

Mohammad Shah Gajjar

In Tabriz, some people had formed a group called the National Assembly. Their cause is freedom; they want to fight the shah.

Hajji Agha comes to Howard one day with the latest news. The Russian consul, Pakhntyanoph, has asked the Russian government to send troops to Tabriz. The whole city is in an uproar. They don't want any more Russians here; most of the shops have closed.

"They may not open tomorrow - so I brought you some hot bread," Hajji Agha explains.

This is grim news indeed, and Howard wants to know more. But Hajji Agha is reluctant to say more. He doesn't want to alarm Howard more than he already has. And he does not want Howard to become frightened and go home, because Hajji Agha has developed a deep affection for his teacher.

Howard wants very much to be of assistance. But he hardly knows what will be most effective. He feels that when the opportunity presents itself, he will seize it.

A few days later, Howard learns that the Iranian foreign ministry has sent a telegram to the National Assembly, informing members that after negotiations among the Russian, English, and Turkish consuls and the Iranian government, the Turks have decided to withdraw from Iran.

The news is greeted with relief by the people of Tabriz.

* * *

Howard has, by now, adopted the local modes of greeting. He places his hand on his heart and bows slightly. This wins him friends as well.

The traditional tea houses are Howard's favorite places.

Generally, there is a choice of seating. One can sit either on the Persian rug-covered flat wooden couches scattered around, which are used also as tables, or at a Western-style chair and table.

Sardar with his friends and followers

Sattar Khan (Sardar) smoking a waterpipe a tea house in Tabriz

Customers sit, inside and outside eating, drinking tea, or smoking water-pipes, "hookahs." The wooden couches are much more popular than the chairs and tables. Some of the couches have low fences around. Them with openings that allow one to enter only at the front. People like to lean against the fences. Howard enjoys watching the preparation of the hookahs. Usually there are several hookahs outside near a small pool or close to the water. The water in the hookahs is changed every time it is served anew. This ensures its freshness. One might also eat a dish called abghosht. This is made of meat, two kinds of beans, tomatoes, potatoes, and many spices and is customarily eaten with plain yogurt, hot bread, pickles, fresh onions, and vegetables. Fresh onions, a must, are served on the side. The tea houses are also famous for their delicious scrambled eggs Almost everyone smokes aftermeals.

Howard and Helen are standing before a tea house one day when Howard sees Hajji Agha in the street, chatting with two men. One of them is carrying an old rifle, and has an ammunition belt hung over his shoulder, covering his back and chest. Howard would come to know this man later. He is Ali Musio.

Ali Musio

A solo performance called "naghaly" is under way in the tea house. The performer chants the story of an Iranian warrior whose figure is painted on one wall of the tea house; the painting depicts a battle scene. The singer, or reciter, periodically makes passionate gestures in the direction of the painting with his pointer, a long wooden stick. Outside and within the tea house, customers sit smoking water pipes as they follow the man's movements.

Howard is intrigued by the performance. A man asks him to

accompany him inside. Helen has her reservations but Howard smiles and takes Helen's hand and follows. The man cleans a large wooden bench covered by a Persian rug in front of the tea house. Howard and Helen sit on each side of a couch. Howard tries to sit cross-legged like the locals, but he still finds it difficult. Someone demonstrates alternate positions, and Howard tries them all. Several curious customers and some pedestrians stop to watch him. Another man places two cups of tea before them, and a large cup of sugar cubes.

Howard and Helen are conscious of an air of great friendliness about them. They seem to be surrounded by smiling faces. Helen's presence has aroused no adverse comment. In those days, women had to cover themselves from head to toe and could not sit among men, especially if the men were not relatives. Evidently an exception has been made for Helen.

Howard has heard that this practice came to Iran with Islam. In those rough old days, the veil, "chador," was used originally to help protect women from rape and abduction. But the chador had evolved. It had become a symbol of the wearer's modesty and the purity of her spiritual convictions.

Howard looks up and notices the performer is staring at him. It is a friendly but very meaningful look.

Howard is plied with more food: eggs, *abghosht*, onions, fresh vegetables, and plain yogurt. The air thickens with smoke from many water pipes. Howard's host watches him intently. Howard is reminded of the way his grandmother watched him eat something made especially for him. It comes to him that this is perhaps their way of welcoming him, of making him feel one of them.

The men exhort Howard to eat and drink; they speak to him in Turkish. When they finally realize he does not understand, they act out their words, to the accompaniment of warm smiles.

Entering the spirit of the moment, Helen also encourages Howard to eat. Young men in Tabriz eat competitively; it's a test of their manhood. They are playing this game with Howard now.

Howard grabs a large piece of bread and piles it with eggs, *abghosht*, and onions to make a huge sandwich. He eats his sandwich and then drinks all the tea on the table. The audience roars its approval. A middle-aged man hands him a fresh water pipe. Howard looks at it hesitantly. A man demonstrates its use. Howard finds all this funny, but he senses the warmth under it all. He smokes, splutteringly at first, but soon gets used to it. Several middle-aged men begin to smoke with Howard. This, too, is a sign of affection and regard. Some of them begin to show off for Howard; they inhale deeply and hold their breath. One short, thin man wearing a hand-embroidered cap blows smoke rings of many different shapes. Another smokes four pipes simultaneously. Howard tries to imitate everyone. There is a great deal of friendly banter and laughter, and shaking of Howard's hand. Howard is made to feel as if he were a long-lost friend.

A man turns to Howard. "American? No Russian . . . ?"

"No Russian! American!"

The man looks around and then spits on the ground, "Russian murderer . . ."

The performer is now shouting himself hoarse. He swings his stick up into the air and catches it with a dramatic flourish. He points to the painting. The end of the pointer is aimed directly at a young boy's face in the painting. He is wearing a traditional hat and playing a drum. Howard is startled to discover that the boy in the painting is the exact double of the chubby-faced drummer boy in the village massacre. And the boy in the painting seems to be staring directly at Howard, just like the blind boy in the village.

As some people prepare to ask about Howard's interest in the painting, there is the sound of mounted men galloping by. They are a troop of Russian cavalry. In their haste they pay no heed to anything in their path. They trample everything before them.

There are gunshots in the distance, then silence, broken only by the sound of horses' hooves. A crowd of people, among them Howard and Helen, set off in the direction of the gunshots. More mounted Russians ride past in the same direction.

They arrive to find several Russian soldiers gripping their rifles tightly, standing over a corpse. A few feet away, a Russian sits inside a carriage, holding a white flag and smoking a cigar. The dead man is a shop owner. His shop is torched. Not a word is said in the watching crowd.

Howard turns to Helen. "Who is that man?"

A familiar voice answers, "The Russian consul." The ubiquitous Hajji Agha. "The dead man has taken a white Russian flag off the door of his neighbor, and he has been punished for this action."

Helen explains the significance of the white flags. "If you hang a white flag over your door, that means you are under the protection of the Russians. And if anyone harms you or removes the flag, they have to face the consequences."

Familiar feelings of outrage and helplessness sweep through Howard. The local government is helpless. He knows that. Russians have friends in high places. The shah is taking orders from the Russians. They prop up his rule in Tabriz.

A young man, a boy almost, breaks through the crowd and kneels beside the corpse. Howard recognizes him: one of his students. He learns later that the dead man is his student's father. As he weeps beside his dead father, the Russian soldiers kick and drag him away.

Howard cannot bear more. He moves in between the young

boy and the soldiers, determined to protect him. The Russian consul is surprised. He fixes Howard with a long, hard stare. But Howard and Hajji Agha are allowed to lead their friend away.

Hajji Agha speaks through gritted teeth, "I'll take him home. If I could I would kill the bastard with my own bare hands."

Other shopkeepers begin to close their stores. Helen and Howard walk down another street. It is filled with angry men. Some carry rifles. Howard senses that something else has happened.

Later that day, he is enlightened by Hajji Agha. "They received a telegram from Tehran saying the shah decided to close down the Parliament. That is it. The Parliament was our only hope."

Chapter Three
Tactics Meet Tabriz

Tabriz has known no calm since Howard's arrival. The tension in the city rises and falls, rises and falls, as in a chess game.

One cool night, Howard, Helen and Mr. Wilson set off for the American consul's residence. They have been invited to a party in celebration of the consul's birthday. A friendship of sorts has formed between W.-F. Doty, the consul, and Mr. Wilson. Mr. Wilson is not an enthusiastic party-goer. He prefers the intimacy of his family and close friends.

The well-appointed carriages outside the consul's house and the fashionably dressed crowd are in sharp contrast with the unpretentious Mission School carriage and its occupants.

Inside the house, Mr. Doty waves his fat cigar in welcome. His house is big and grand; art, American and Persian, is much in evidence. Persian rugs in rich blues, greens, and beige cover the floors. There is laughter and the sound of glasses being filled and refilled. A heavyset man is at the piano.

Mr. Doty's banter is consular, practiced.

"I hope you aren't working our young friend to the bone," he says, laughing and flourishing his huge cigar.

"No," says Mr. Wilson. " No. Not at all."

Many impassioned conversations are in progress. Howard and Helen drift through the room, catching stray bits of political talk. Howard is agog with curiosity. He has many questions. And some, he hopes, conceivably might be answered at this gathering.

Later that evening, Howard finds himself with Mr. Doty, Mr. Wilson, and some distinguished-looking men of Tabriz. They, except for Mr. Wilson, are in various stages of intoxication. They joke feebly. Mr. Wilson is a detached presence in the group. His eyes are half-closed; he seems engrossed in his pipe.

Gunshots are heard. After the inevitable silence, the conversation in Howard's group turns to the subject of Iran's borders. Mr. Wilson very diffidently mentions the behavior of the Russians at the border.

Mr. Doty takes a puff of his cigar; he taps the ashes slowly into a glass. "It all started because of a white horse that belonged to a Russian officer named Doyghlazoph. It went over the border and he followed, without Iranian authority to do so. He killed a shepherd and his son who believed they had caught a wild horse. He was then set upon by an angry mob and killed. Russian soldiers then crossed the border. They razed the customs post and most of the village with it."

Mr. Wilson demurs. "I've been told that the villages of Pelesavar, Shyreensoo, and Javadkandy were also razed. And that they killed everything they could find, even the livestock. And all this over a horse!"

He continues, sipping his drink delicately. "I was also told that the horse was stolen from the hills in Iran by Russian soldiers."

Howard has held his peace until this moment. He cannot

restrain himself any longer, "No, no, no! I saw the whole thing! It was a cold-blooded massacre! There was a horse, it is true. And a young boy. And a blind boy." He pauses "It happened the day I arrived. I was passing through the village."

The ensuing silence doesn't last long. Howard returns passionately to his theme. "I am confused. Would someone please explain why the Iranian government is so passive? The ownership of the horse is irrelevant. What happened out there was murder. And more than murder. It was a massacre."

Mr. Doty stirs uncomfortably in his seat.

But Howard is in no mood to relent. "I am sure, Mr. Doty, that you have an opinion. Perhaps you could tell us what to make of the situation."

Mr. Doty is evasive. "What situation?"

Howard is on the verge of losing his temper, "This situation. The gunshots. The fighting, the bloodshed. How will it end?"

Mr. Wilson and Doty look at each other. Clearly Mr. Doty doesn't want to be involved in such a conversation. He extinguishes his cigar and turns wearily to Howard. "Mr. Baskerville, this is the East. These are their politics."

He sips his whisky moodily.

But Howard has the bit between his teeth, "I see that. But you say nothing about who is responsible. You say nothing about colonialism, Mr. Doty."

Mr. Doty smiles, "Ah, yes, colonialism. When you are young and ambitious, the world seems a simple place. But the good are seldom as good as one thinks; and neither are the bad as bad. I expect you'll learn that for yourself."

Howard looks enraged.

"But now," says Mr. Doty, rising a little unsteadily to his feet, "I must attend to my other guests. This has been a most interesting conversation. Thank you."

One of the Americans breaks the silence. "I hear the English and the Russians have come to an agreement. They have told the shah they will support him and help him defeat the movement of the people."

As if on cue, another American says, "It seems we are the only ones who don't meddle in the affairs of other countries. That is something to be proud of. But Howard, I hear you have found love. It's a long way to come for it, isn't it?"

These remarks are greeted with raucous laughter. Mr. Wilson, unnoticed, has left the group.

Howard is seething when he is joined by Helen. She wants him to dance with her. He rages silently all evening.

* * *

Howard's friendship with Mr. Sharifzadeh is deepening. They meet regularly and lend each other books. Howard is teaching Mr. Sharifzadeh about America, and Mr. Sharifzadeh is helping Howard understand Iranian culture and history.

Helen watches these developments. She worries that Howard may be letting his natural goodness and passion carry him into dangerous areas. His reading lamp is on late into the night. He looks tired much of the time.

* * *

Mount Sahand dominates Tabriz. Howard was enchanted by the mountains around Tabriz from the very beginning. He and Helen often picnic there. They like to hear the wind soughing through the trees. Howard can't help thinking there is something otherworldly about these mountains.

The breeze that comes down from the mountain talks to you. It whispers secrets and meanings in a language that cannot be deciphered by the human ear.

"Why here?" Howard and Helen are walking in a meadow below the mountains.

Howard does not understand the question.

"Here," Helen says. "Tabriz. What brought you here to Tabriz?"

Howard keeps his eyes on the slopes above him, "God sent me. Well, that, and I kept getting refused everywhere else."

He notices Helen is interested, and so he goes on. "I was on my way to becoming a minister back home, but I didn't want to stay there. I needed to leave, to spread my wings, so to speak. That's when I came to realize that I could use my education as a way to travel–see the world, you know. China refused me, Malaysia refused me, and Egypt had no use for me. But Iran."

He turns to Helen. "Iran accepted me. This may not have been my first choice, but maybe it was God's choice for me. Now, I'm here to be a teacher and a minister."

"Were you ever sanctioned by a church for ministry?"

"Never. But being a minister is more than wearing a collar or standing on a platform before a congregation or being ordained by a specific church. It's all about what's inside of you. It's about helping those who need to be helped and following blindly where God leads you."

Howard notices a white horse parading across the valley. He gets to his feet. "I may be only a teacher to these people, but I feel I am here for a much greater purpose. A purpose I don't even know."

"What a beautiful horse," he says, "I'm going to chat with him."

He approaches the horse, holding an apple out before him. Helen follows him nervously.

The horse takes a bite of the apple, as Howard strokes him.

Helen, surprised, comes closer. "I can't believe he's so gentle."

"I think I'd like to take him for a ride," says Howard.

"Howard, it's a wild horse; they're dangerous."

"Are you afraid because he's wild or because he's a horse?"

"You know I'm scared of riding horses."

"There is nothing to be scared of. It's simple, just like this."

He walks to the side of the horse. "You have to talk to them first . . ." He whispers something in the horse's ear. "You have to make them your friend . . ." He strokes the side of the horse. "Then you gently mount them."

Howard gets on the horse cautiously. When he feels secure, he raises his arms slowly as if he were a great warrior.

"Then you are part of them." Howard leans over the horse's ear. "And you have to keep talking to them."

Howard whispers something in the horse's ear again.

Suddenly, the horse whinnies and takes off. Horse and rider disappear over a small hill. When Helen reaches the crest of the hill, she sees a muddy Howard picking himself up off the ground. His face is covered with mud. As he wipes the mud from his eyes, the riderless horse disappears into the mountains.

"Perhaps you should have spoken to him in English," Helen says, laughing.

Before going back down to the city, Howard turns to take a last look at the mountains. He sees the horse standing on top of the mountain. He remembers the white horse at the border.

* * *

Hajji Agha wants Howard to visit his house but has been too shy to ask. One day he takes Howard some fresh hot bread.

They stand outside the cottage. Howard notices two horses standing nearby, one white, the other brown.

Hajji Agha smiles, "I thought you might enjoy a ride."

On the way back, Hajji Agha musters up the courage to invite Howard to a wedding at his house.

"The invitation is for Miss Helen too, of course."

To Hajji Agha's delight, Howard accepts immediately. But riding home, Hajji Agha worries about his father. The invitation had been made without his father's knowledge. That night, he tells him, stammeringly. His father laughs loudly and says that, of course, Hajji Agha was quite right to invite Howard. He would be honored by Howard's presence.

The house is palatial, many-roomed. Howard is reminded of hotels at home. Fruit trees and flower beds surround it. Out front from which is a pool, a giant sprinkler shoots water into the air, as high as the second story.

More than fifteen enormous cooking pots are set in a back corner. Several cooks are at work. A troupe of traditional musicians is playing. Helen is escorted indoors by a group of girls. They pass through two beautifully carved wooden doors. Howard and Hajji Agha follow. Helen and Howard are led away in different directions from the giant hallway.

There are patterns and pictures painted on tiles and plaster work, which are scattered throughout the ceiling and the walls through the hallway. There is mirror work throughout the house.

Helen disappears into a group of women. They ply her with food. Young girls play with her hair; she is hugged and kissed. Attempts at conversation are made.

Hajji Agha escorts Howard to a large room that contains more than five hundred men. At Howard's entrance, they all rise in welcome. They remain standing until Hajji Agha's father's formal welcome to Howard has been made. Hajji Agha's father walks Howard around the room, performing introductions

They sit beside two tall windows that overlook the yard a provide a breathtaking view of the mountains, out and Howard takes it in. He notices they have brand-new cushions for him to sit on. He is very impressed and is amazed by all the rugs surrounding them. Some are fifty yards long, and many others hang on the wall. They are like large paintings, each depicting a different scene. One has three birds; there is also a battle scene and a hunting scene as well.

A man brings a water pipe for Hajji Agha′s father and one for Howard. The sight of Howard drawing on a water-pipe delights Hajji Agha′s father. He turns to his son. ″Tell Mr. Howard that we are happy to have him here. He is welcome anytime.″

Howard now knows a few Farsi words. He thanks Hajji Agha's father for his hospitality.

A smiling elderly man declares, "Tell him he is welcome in

everyone's heart and home." Almost everyone has a gift for Howard, or offers him something: dishes, objects of art, Persian rugs, and Iranian traditional clothes.

In the other room now, Helen is dressed in colorful native wear and dancing with a group of women. Two older women play on traditional instruments; another dances. Helen, too, is being given presents. Some teach her how to dance as the bride watches.

It is time to serve dinner. Twenty men set out food and utensils. A long, narrow piece of material is laid all the way from one end of the room to the other. It takes eight such pieces to cover the whole room. Just these preparations for the meal take more than thirty minutes.

Hajji Agha's father has had the chefs prepare five main different dishes and at least ten different side dishes. Everyone around Howard plies him with food. In Iran, you let your guests know that you are happier if they eat more.

Hajji Agha makes several vain attempts to restrain Howard's neighbors. They tell him to explain to Howard that "among us it is not good to eat so little." They wonder if Howard is, perhaps, just shy.

"We are all good eaters here," one man says, "eat more." Hajji Agha translates for Howard what the older men say. Howard laughs and begins to heap food on his neighbors' plates. Everyone is laughing. The men speak Farsi to Howard; he replies in English and broken Farsi. The meal ends. The wedding continues with music being performed for the groom and guests by the montreb, which are the traditional band members and their instruments. It is followed by ten kinds of pastries platters full of fruits for dessert are brought out, and, of course, plenty of tea.

Howard and Helen are made to feel completely at home. They return to the school compound in a state of elation.

* * *

Howard walks into his classroom and immediately notices that every Iranian student is wearing a black shirt. And so are some of the Americans. He turns to Hajji Agha for answers.

The expression on Hajji Agha's face is grim. "A few days ago," he says in a trembling voice, "the Russians crossed the border. They attacked more than ten villages. They killed everything they found, even the animals. And they burned all the villages to the ground."

He points to an empty chair, the chubby-faced boy's. "They killed him, too. He was just playing his drum."

Howard is overwhelmed by grief. He remembers the intentness of the boy's stare. He remembers that the chubby-faced boy was killed on the day of his arrival. How, then, could he be killed again? He is filled with confusion. He just stares; he has no answers but many questions. The mystery of the chubby-faced boy grows. For Howard, it is becoming, increasingly, a mystical matter. It is something new for Howard and, for the moment at least, inexplicable. He feels haunted by the boy's ghost.

* * *

Howard learns soon afterward that Hajji Agha and some boys gathering donations for the villagers who had survived the massacre. Here, he thinks, is my chance.

The next day is Sunday. The church is full of the usual crowd. Most of those in attendance had planned dances or barbecues or card parties for later that day. Howard had been preoccupied all morning, and during church. This does not escape Helen's notice.

The choir is singing. But Howard's attention is elsewhere. He feels drawn towards the statue of Jesus. He feels Jesus's eyes are moving. He gets up and walks towards the statue. He stops beside the dais. The choir is still singing. But everyone's attention is on Howard. Now, Howard sees Jesus's lips moving but he can't hear his voice. Howard ascends the dais; several choir members make room for him. He walks past them and stops underneath the statue. The church is very silent.

He kneels under the statue. The Reverend Vanneman raises his arms and asks for complete silence. A loud crash of thunder breaks Howard's concentration. He looks about him. He is extremely embarrassed.

The Reverend Vanneman puts his arm around Howard's shoulder. He lifts Howard's face up toward his and asks, "Are you blessed, my son?"

Howard says nothing at first. He is too overcome. When he speaks, his words come out in a whisper, "I am fine. I am fine. It just doesn't feel right." Then he gets to his feet. As he walks away, his voice rises, "It just doesn't feel right. We are missionaries. We ought to be out there helping all those burned villages! I am in jail behind these walls hiding from the truth." He walks out of the church, followed by Helen.

Howard′s actions strike many of the churchgoers as odd, possibly unbalanced. But even they couldn′t deny his force and the truth in his words. He had forced them to face unpleasant facts: their safety, which they tried to pass off as high-minded neutrality; the suffering in the city. He is, of course, resented by some people. Others, after thinking it over, decide that he is right.

″I′m going to do it, Helen.″ Getting water from the well, by the church, Howard turns to Helen. "I'm going to do what I can."

Many exit the church and look at them with concern and a few walk to Howard and reach out to shake his hand. Soon, aided by Helen and Hajji Agha, he organizes a relief expedition. The group, led by Howard and Hajji Agha, reaches a hill above one of the razed villages.

Below them lies a world laid waste. The smell of scorched flesh is overpowering. Covering their faces, they ride down to the burnt-out village. Howard has seen such scenes before. The blind drummer-boy's face rises again in his memory. Now, his presence is palpable. Howard sees a piece of burnt drum lying on the ground. But before he can reach it, a young man bends down and picks it up. He rubs it thoughtfully before stowing it away in his pocket.

They ride to the next village and, incredibly, hear sounds of revelry. Nearby, a wedding is in progress. Howard's students begin to distribute the supplies they have brought.

The villagers insist on their attendance. The group settles down to watch. The groom is paraded around the village. Music is playing, and the entire village is dancing. People are gathered on rooftops and in trees. Many celebrants dance in front of the groom; some throw candy over his head to wish the groom and his bride a good and sweet life in the future. The kids run around, trying to collect the candy, and people welcome the groom with sweet drinks. More men join the dance.

One of the musicians plays a large drum, the *dohoul*; it hangs on his shoulder and is played with small sticks. Others play an instrument called the *soze*; this is something like a saxophone. The sounds created by the *soze* and *dohoul* can carry as far as a mile.

There is a unique style of wedding ceremony in Iran. The groom is taken to a bathhouse; male relatives and friends join him. In those days, there were one to three public bathhouses located within the villages. From dawn to about eight in the morning, they were open for the males, and after that, the women took over and no men were allowed. But when there was a wedding, the bathhouse opened at a special time for the groom and his entourage. When the groom is done with his bath, he exits the bathhouse. The Motreb are waiting for him. They play and dance all the way to his house. As they walk, they will frequently stop to talk to friends and dance in the streets through the village. They cheer for him all the way home; sometimes this goes on for miles.

The bride also goes through the same ritual. When she is brought to her new husband's house, her dowry, known as *jahaz*, is brought with her, usually on the backs of donkeys but sometimes by people, to the accompaniment of the Motreb.

At the time of the actual wedding, the whole village comes out to watch, serving food, dancing, and celebrating. Generally, most of the village is invited, and the party continues through the night until they send the bride and groom into their private room, decorated especially for their first night. The Motreb also plays music through the night and, after performing a comic play, sends the new couple off.

An older man approaches Howard and asks him to dance. Howard gets off his horse. A couple of the missionaries look disapproving. He does an unskillful imitation of what he has seen. Children laugh at him, and several adults try to teach him.

Then, two mounted men ride up to the group; they speak in urgent voices to several older men. Panic sets in instantly.

Hajji Agha canters up beside Howard. "We have to leave right away."

Gunfire is heard. Howard turns to Hajji Agha.

"It is a warlord, Shojaeh Nezam. He's merciless. Get on your horse, Howard. Please." Howard mounts his horse and they set off.

They come across some of Shojaeh Nezam's men. They are an assortment of Turks, Kurds, and Lores. Howard sees an elderly woman cautiously remove her flowerpots from the windowsill as the last of the doors and windows shut throughout the village.

Helen notices that Howard is not with the group. He has stopped behind a tree, watching. Hajji Agha joins him. He is badly frightened. They watch a weeping elderly woman holding on weakly to one of her chickens. A man pushes her into a small creek; another man strikes a villager who is attempting to defend his Persian rug. The rug owner is beaten badly. An elderly man, wearing a ripped shirt, is thrown into a freezing pond. He, too, is bleeding badly and seems to have lost consciousness.

Shojaeh Nezam Marandy, a portly man with a thick mustache, sits on a nearby balcony and puffs on his large golden water pipe (hookah).

Shojaeh Nezam with his son in Tabriz

Shojaeh Nezam with his ruthless men.

Having retrieved the elderly man from the pond, Shojaeh Nezam's men prepare to hang him from a tree. Howard's eyes are locked on the elderly man, who is struggling to breathe. Abruptly, Howard jumps on his horse and, taking a white flag from one of the carriages, rides out into the open.

Shojaeh Nezam rises, amazed. Nervous, but implacably loyal, Hajji Agha fearfully follows Howard. The brigand's gunmen point their rifles toward the two of them. They await Shojaeh Nezam's command to shoot, but he raises his hand to stay them. Howard cuts the rope around the elderly man's neck. He turns to Hajji Agha. "Tell him I will pay for the old man's life."

The motionless old man falls into Howard's arms. Weak with fear, Hajji Agha conveys Howard's message.

The brigand fixes Howard with a piercing look. "Who is this man?" he shouts.

"An American teacher." Hajja Agha thinks quickly. "He used to be head of the American Army. He works for the American embassy as well." He realizes that he has the brigand's attention, "He is a Christian missionary; they all are."

Hajji Agha turns to Howard. "Do you know what you're doing?"

"Tell him I am taking the old man. Tell him to tell his men to leave us alone. He won't embarrass himself by killing an unarmed man."

Hajji Agha replies, "That will not work here."

"Especially if I am his guest. He would not dishonor himself by killing his guest."

"Good, that is better."

"And ask him how much he wants for the old man."

Hajji Agha cautiously translates Howard's words.

Shojaeh Nezam grins ominously.

The whole missionary team is surrounded by the warlord's men, who are methodically looting them. They are terrified, and deeply resentful of Howard's actions. But they can only watch silently.

Howard covers the old man with his jacket. He leads his horse by its reins; Hajji Agha follows close behind. A shot rings out. The elderly man drops to the ground, pulling down Howard with him.

Howard sees Shojaeh Nezam looming over him. His rifle is still smoking. Shojaeh Nezam looks over at Hajji Agha. "Tell him," he says coldly, "he can have the old man for free. Your American friend is alive only because he is a brave man."

Howard gets on his horse. He understands the unuttered threat in the man's words. No one says a word all the way home.

* * *

A few days later, Howard and Helen go to their favorite bread shop. Here, bread is baked three times a day. The shopkeeper saves the freshest loaves for his best customers.

After choosing his loaves, Howard picks some small pieces of stone out of them. He is still amused by the way bread is baked in this country. The dough is placed in a cavernous muddy oven with a large hole in the front. Small, clean rocks are scattered inside; the fires burn in the back of the oven and make the rocks extremely hot. The dough is cooked on the hot rocks; the bread is hung on racks all over the walls and over the counter.

Howard has chosen a couple of loaves of cold flat bread at the local bakery. He puts his money on the scale. The shop owner takes the cold bread away from him and replaces it with three hot ones. He refuses payment for them. He puts the money back inside Howard's pocket with a smile. When Howard tries again to pay him, he comes around the counter, hugs Howard, and pushes him gently out of the store.

Howard used to catch cold often. Mr. Sharifzadeh had introduced him to an herbal drink, a potent remedy. Such herbal cures were many generations old; each generation handed down its discoveries to the next, and the people relied on them as we do on our doctors today. Howard is becoming something of an expert creating different concoctions for his ailments.

The shop that sells herbs is their next stop. The owner, Yar Mohammad, gives Howard a huge hug when he and Helen enter. Waving his arms around his packed shop, he tells Howard to take whatever he needs. Howard makes several complicated choices. He carries his herbs to the front counter and places them on the scale to be weighed. He places some money on the other side of the scale. Yar Mohammad returns in haste from a back room, carrying a handful of fresh herbs. He puts Howard's herbs and his fresh herbs in to a bag and hands it to Howard. He pushes the money back toward him. Howard tries to force the money on the man but it is of no use. Yar Mohammad stuffs the money in Howard's pocket, and smilingly gestures them out of the shop.

Howard and Helen notice that everyone bows to them as they pass by. Howard returns their bows, his hand on his heart.

Helen is nervous about Howard's deepening involvement in local life. But she also likes it. It seems the right thing to do. He is brave and generous. Nevertheless, she is worried. But she keeps her worries to herself.

* * *

It is the next day, and after classes have ended Howard leaves the building. Many students, instead of going home as usual, seem to be waiting for him. Every young face before him is smiling. The plump Hussein Khan starts clapping slowly. The others follow with loud cheering and sustained applause.

Mr. Sharifzadeh, who is standing nearby, says, "My young friend, you have become their lion, their Lion of God."

Mr. Wilson is standing with a group of teachers on his balcony. Wright, an American, is one of them. He clearly does not share the general admiration for Howard.

Mr. Sharifzadeh is in a hurry. He embraces Howard warmly before leaving.

Howard, although grateful for all the warmth directed his way, is embarrassed and uncomfortable. Casting a vague, shy smile around, he leaves.

* * *

Hajji Agha goes to the telegraph office every day for news from Tehran and other cities. He passes every piece of his information to Howard. The news coming into the telegraph office is confidential, but nothing is held from Mr. Sharifzadeh. He, too, is a source of information for Howard.

Howard's curiosity is exceptional. Hajji Agha reflects that no foreigner known to him, or anyone else, has ever taken such an interest in local affairs. It makes him feel very close to his young teacher.

Late one afternoon, Howard is boiling herbs for tea; he hardly drinks coffee anymore. He is deep in thought when he hears a knock at the door. It is Hajji Agha holding two loaves of fresh, hot bread. And he has also brought an invitation from Mr. Sharifzadeh.

The smell of the borage herbs fills Howard's little cottage.

"We should go; we must not be late for the sheikh," says Hajji Agha, who doesn't really like the herbal drinks he is offered.

"I don't know the word. What does sheikh mean?"

"Man of God,' one who leads the people to freedom and prosperity. It is a nickname for people like Mr. Sharifzadeh. Of course, in the past, they used to call philosophers and great poets, 'sheikh.' But that was long ago. There are almost no sheikhs left now."

* * *

In order to understand the path Howard chose in Tabriz, one must first understand Mr. Sharifzadeh and his influence on Howard. There is a big difference between Mr. Sharifzadeh and the other clergymen. He is really more philosopher than clergyman. Those who know him well are reminded of Jalal L-Din Rumi or Omar Khayyam, philosopher-poets. Mr. Sharifzadeh is exceptionally independent-minded. Most of the time, he does not even wear a clergyman's attire. He says that dressing up in a turban and long overcoat isn't a requirement in Islam.

The practice has its origins in respect for the prophet Mohammad, the messenger of God. Mohammad lived in the hot lands of Saudi Arabia where a turban and long overcoat keeps the body cool and protected. To dress like an Arab man thus came to be an Islamic tradition. But then the clergy converted it into a rigid rule. Mr. Sharifzadeh's independence of mind does not endear him to the clergy, many of whom are fanatics.

Mr. Sharifzadeh is dedicated to learning. He has come to understand that one has to open one's mind to the ideas of others; only thus can one learn more oneself. He teaches that one must not believe in the superiority of one's own ideas. That way lies hatred and destruction. Most people are ignorant of their own natures and the true meaning of religion. Religion should never be used as a tool to gain power. His ideas run contrary to most of the clergy, who believe that to be so open is to violate one's soul and spirit; it is to dishonor one's religious heritage. But, Mr. Sharifzadeh contends, to be a decent human being, one must learn to love and not to hate, to build and not destroy, to heal and not to harm. All religions have this in common; one finds the truth within oneself by finding God. And Mr. Sharifzadeh practices all that he believes. He is a man of very high principles.

Muslim and Christian, Mr. Sharifzadeh and Howard become friends because they have such ideas in common. They remain devoted to each other until the end. Each is interested in what the other can teach him. Mr. Sharifzadeh want to know about America. He wants to know everything. He wishes to someday travel to America and see everything for himself. He thinks America is the only truly democratic country. He says that America is the highway for democracy, a free society for the scientists of the world.

But Mr. Sharifzadeh also has a winning sense of humor. He always puts a smile on Howard's face. He loves to travel and encourages others to do so. He believes that by exploring the whole world, people will understand their own corner of it more clearly. If one finds something good in another culture, adopt it and make it your own. He is, in his way, Howard often thinks, an ideal American.

* * *

Howard and Hajji Agha get out of the carriage and walk upto Mr. Sharifzadeh's house. Mr. Sharifzadeh's helper leads them inside.

In Iran, one always enters a large yard first; there is a pool in the middle and lots of trees scattered Around the building or main house. There is usually a large balcony in the front with a view of the neighborhood.

Howard and Hajji Agha follow Mr. Sharifzadeh's helper up some stairs and across a long balcony into Mr. Sharifzadeh's room.

Mr. Sharifzadeh has just finished praying. His feet are unshod; a long white robe is wrapped around his trim body. He speaks softly. "Please come in. I am very happy to see you." They sit together at the same end of the room, on the floor, and lean against the soft cushions.

He turns to Howard, with the kind smile that inspires such affection and devotion in the young man. "You are very welcome here, Mr. Howard. Your company makes us happy."

"I am very happy to be here, Mr. Sheikh."

"Mr. Howard, this word 'sheikh' must not come from you. I cannot be a sheikh."

"Mr. Sharifzadeh, you must forgive me if the word gives offense. Ignorance, not impertinence, is the cause. But would you, if it isn't discourteous of me to ask, tell me what the word means?"

This has to pass through the filter of Hajji Agha's translation. That takes time. Mr. Sharifzadeh listens intently

"Mr. Howard, the word 'sheikh,' in Western culture, would mean a priest - a holy man. The sheikh also cannot accept any social position or nickname. He must be knowledgeable and wise so that people can discuss every kind of problem with him. A sheikh, however, must live for the eternal truth and must not desire material goods of any kind. People like Rumi, Omar Khayyam, Hafez, Saddi, Shams: they were sheikhs. I am far from being one."

Hajji Agha's services are required again.

"But Mr. Sharifzadeh," Howard says, "you have all these qualifications."

Mr. Sharifzadeh looks first at Hajji Agha, then at Howard.

"Most important, people cannot choose or accept a sheikh. It is the sheikh who chooses the people. Please just call me by my name, Sharifzadeh."

Mr. Sharifzadeh has been handling a string of prayer beads throughout their conversation. Howard has observed this many times elsewhere in Tabriz. He asks Mr. Sharifzadeh about the practice.

"It keeps the thought of God before man at all times."

"You mean you cannot remember God without them?"

Mr. Sharifzadeh laughs. "Yes, you can. They are tools, a religious symbol. Just like that cross that you wear around your neck."

Howard smiles. They have much in common. They are both free spirits. They both believe all men are born free and must live free. That we all have free will. That people must be free to think and say what is on their minds.

Mr. Sharifzadeh is curious about the American Constitution and the system of government. Howard tries his best to explain. Their conversation ranges far and wide and the hours pass.

It is after midnight when Howard and Hajji Agha rise to leave. Howard notices Mr. Sharifzadeh is not as content as he was when they arrived. He is worried that he has said something to upset him. He relaxes a little when Mr. Sharifzadeh reaches out and embraces him. Howard is surprised to see tears falling from Mr. Sharifzadeh's eyes. Hajji Agha is surprised by the tears. Mr. Sharifzadeh walks his guests to the yard and says goodnight. Howard looks back and sees him walking toward the pool in the yard.

* * *

The friendship between Howard and Mr. Sharifzadeh deepens rapidly. Howard feels he can bring up any subject with him. The place of women in Iran has been occupying his thoughts. The practice of wearing veils mystifies him. Women always walked behind the men they are with; he thinks they are treated like social inferiors.

He raises the subject one day in a tea house. He notices Mr. Sharifzadeh watching a couple of women passing by. A scarf falls from a woman's head; a little boy picks it up, and runs with it to the lady.

"I have wanted to ask you about something for a long time,

but . . . ″ He falters.

"Tell me. What is it? What would you like to know?"

"You must forgive me, Mr. Sharifzadeh. May I give an offering. I feel sorry for the women here. They seem to me prisoners within their own families. They are treated like slaves. They have no right to go to school and cannot take on any social responsibility. I am sorry, sir. I have to say this behavior toward women is inhuman."

"Our religion does not permit women to do many things, this is true. We do not believe some things are proper; women must be protected the same way they are within your religion, but you choose to be blinded by the similarities. The fact is, none of what you said is permitted by Islam or any other religion. Yes, women's rights have been abused throughout history, but through the fault of men, power-mad dictators, and misunderstood religious beliefs. Here, when a woman becomes a mother, she becomes a channel to the future, for our traditions. Our mothers are as close to God as is possible. Therefore, men see it as their duty to take care of women and support them. But men do, of course, abuse tradition; kindness and respect all too easily become oppression. Howard, our society is behind compared to the rest of the world, and it is not entirely our fault. Here, no one really has a choice - man or woman. We are all slaves of this society. Man must first achieve political freedom, and then we can work on personal freedoms and become whole."

"Why don't you speak out? People will listen to you." Mr. Sharifzadeh is silent for a long time. When he speaks, his voice is full of deeply felt emotion. "Changing misguided beliefs in people is ten times harder than overthrowing a tyrant. Besides, everything has its time. It would not be possible now. People are poor and hungry and have to feed themselves first. It is a slow process, and we have to win our liberties first."

* * *

Howard's friendship with Mr. Sharifzadeh deepens. They meet regularly and lend each other books. Howard teaches Mr. Sharifzadeh about America, and Mr. Sharifzadeh helps Howard understand Iranian culture and history. Soon it dawns on Howard that Mr. Sharifzadeh is one of the intellectual forces behind the people's movement for freedom, one of the authors of the constitution that created the movement. He is a scholar who loves not only books but also the world outside his study.

Howard, Mr.Sharifzadeh and Hajji Agha ride often in the hills around the city. During these rides, their conversations range widely. Howard learns about the invidious agreement between the Russians and the English to divide Iran between them. England is to control the south and Russia the north and Tehran.

Howard neither likes nor accepts Russian or British involvement in Iran, although he understands their selfish motives. But he is confused about the Iranian government's betrayal of its own people. That is why, Mr. Sharifzadeh and other freedom fighters gain respect in Howard's mind and heart.

He recognizes that they have no formal training or military organization or any modern weapons. Yet they seek to overcome the Russians, the English, and the shah's own Royal Army. Their goal seems impossible.

But then he remembers reading about how Cyrus the Great defeated Babylon. He studies Iranian cultures and history constantly and now knows Iranian history well. After all, he was a history teacher.

One day he is so taken by the events in Tabriz that he reminds his student about their great history. And what was better than how Cyrus the Great captured the ancient city of Opis? And this is the story that he tells:

In Opis, which today is in central Iraq, north of Baghdad, the Babylonians had built a tall and seemingly impenetrable wall on the city's northern limits. They called it the dam of Mody or the dam of Bakhton-nassr. Around the wall they dug a deep ditch and across it built a wooden bridge. If attacked, the Babylonians could destroy the bridge to prevent the enemy from entering the city. On the south, Opis was protected by the wide Tigris River. The Babylonians were confident that it was impossible for the Persians to seize the city.

But Cyrus the Great was not happy with the way the leaders treated their people, especially the Jews. Several times the Babylonians had attacked Jerusalem, destroying the city and kidnaping its people. The Jews' only hope was Cyrus the Great, and so they sent a message to him appealing for help. In response, King Cyrus had his men secretly work for a year on to dig hundreds of small channels to drain the water out of the Tigris, upstream of Opis. When all these channels were opened at once, the Tigris River went dry at Opis. Cyrus the Great and his army entered the city on October 12, 539 B.C., by simply walking into the city across the river bed. They conquered the Babylonians so quickly that for several days many of the people of Opis did not know that the city had fallen.

Cyrus ordered his soldiers to treat all with respect. He forgave the defeated leaders and ordered the freedom for all religions. He forbad his soldiers from taking anything from the city.

Cyrus paid special attention to the Jewish people. After he defeated Babylon, he issued this order: "Yahweh, the God of all skies, has given Cyrus all the countries in the earth and asked that a house be built in the land of Jerusalem for Yahweh. Therefore, all Jews may go back to Jerusalem and help to build the house of Yahweh, who is God of Israel. And whoever is unable to go back shall be given expenses and whatever necessary to make the trip."

King Cyrus also ordered rebuilding of the holy temple in Jerusalem that was destroyed by Bakhton-Nassr, and paid the cost from his own government's treasury. He also ordered all gold and silver dishes, which Bakhton-Nassr had brought from the Holy Land, to be returned. As a result of these actions by Cyrus, 42,360 of the Jewish people residing in Babylon returned to Jerusalem. But many decided to join Cyrus the Great. It was there that Cyrus the Great wrote the world first decoration of human rights.

When Howard finishes this story, his students are proud of Cyrus for not only his military victories but his humanitarian rule, and they contrast that with the present government's policies.

Chapter Four

In the Midst of Decision

Howard's interest in local affairs is developing very fast. But Mr. Sharifzadeh had reservations in the beginning. Howard is far from home, and Mr. Sharifzadeh does not want him to forget about his life and his family in America. Howard himself is not aware how powerfully drawn he is to the people's struggle. He is struggling to find his own way, to somehow accommodate the demands of his love for Helen, and his conscience.

Helen has become devoted to Howard. She makes sure that his clothes are always clean, his cottage neat and tidy. Her attentions to him are becoming wifely. Howard tries many times to get her on a horse but to no avail. He had taught Hajji Agha the proper way to ride a horse and to use a rifle, but Helen just watches.

Howard and Mr. Sharifzadeh now meet at the small local tea house. It is a quiet place, and a favorite with both of them. It is smaller than most tea houses but cozy; there is room for about five or six people outside.

The owner is a kind old man called Sheikh Nosrat. He is both owner and the only staff of the tea house. Because he lives in a room in the back of the tea house, it is practically always open. He is a mystic and a philosopher, living detached from the life around him. He very seldom speaks. The minute one sits down, he serves tea and a water pipe. He will not ask or tell you what you want or how much you owe; you have to work it out yourself. Should you forget to pay him, he will not protest. He reveres Mr. Sharifzadeh and shows him many small attentions.

A brook runs in front of the tea house. Several tall trees, covered with snow, loom over the entrance. They canopy the outside patio. The snow in the trees falls softly down, brushing the clothes of the two men. Mr. Sharifzadeh smokes. He watches Howard, who is absorbed by the sight of a snow-coated leaf falling into the water. The leaf is at the mercy of the slow-moving water. It is pushed this way and that before it is allowed to continue downstream. The leaf gets stuck on the left bank with other stranded brethren. A current finally pushes all the leaves forward. But this time, as if they had learned their lesson, they stick together and travel in a herd.

Mr. Sharifzadeh reads Howard's face. He inhales deeply of his water pipe. The sound disrupts Howard's reflections. He turns toward Mr. Sharifzadeh and waits for him to say something, but Mr. Sharifzadeh is silent.

Howard looks reflective. Then, as if he had reached some weighty conclusion, he says, "Before I came here, I had a quite different picture of the Eastern world, especially regarding Iran. I had read novels and stories and travelers' accounts. But I always wanted to see it for myself. I expected tall beautiful women with big brown eyes and long black hair down to their knees. According to my reading, these beauties lived to kiss and cuddle." The memory makes him laugh.

"But it was all fantasy, a fabrication, just a big dream. But some of it must be true. What happened to your country? What happened to all the love, poetry, and beauty?"

Mr. Sharifzadeh plays with his beads silently; he regards the water and the leaves floating upon it.

"My friend," he says, after a long pause, "these people do not always have bread to feed themselves. They are so poor that they have forgotten that they are alive. Now they are filled only with thoughts of struggle and fighting. They are trying to learn how to free themselves from their misery. The people are oppressed. For love to exist, to express love, you must have peace, comfort, and bread. Here love has become an indulgence."

"Have you ever been in love?" It is the most impertinent question he has ever put to Mr.Sharifzadeh. But he speaks the words almost reflexively; he has come to feel so close to Mr. Sharifzadeh that the possibility that he might be giving offense occurs to him only as an afterthought. He waits anxiously.

Mr. Sharifzadeh applies himself to his hookah. He plays with his beads for a long while. Finally, he speaks: "The truth is, I would not have time for it. I have devoted my life to serving the people. But you are still young and fresh. You must listen to your heart before it is too late."

Howard has never mentioned Helen to Mr. Sharifzadeh. Mr. Sharifzadeh's powers of intuition have always impressed him. He wonders what he should say.

But Mr. Sharifzadeh makes it easy for him. "The doubt you are struggling with is nothing more than love for your soulmate."

They are interrupted by Sheikh Nosrat who serves them fresh tea. Mr. Sharifzadeh watches Nosrat return to his corner, prepare his water pipe, and begin to smoke. He turns his attention back to Howard. "Sheikh Nosrat comes from a wealthy family. He had a playmate of the same age; she was the daughter of one of the workers of his family. One day, when young Sheikh Nosrat was playing with his playmate, her father walks up, grabs her hand, and drags her into his house. The father looked very upset. Sheikh Nosrat was puzzled, and no one gave him an explanation. He didn't forget her. He made several unsuccessful attempts to see her. He learned one day that she was engaged to marry a man from another city, and would soon leave the town. So he asked to marry her. But the family would not allow him to marry so far beneath him. He hid on the rooftop every night, all night, for a month, hoping to see her for just a moment. He never did. You must remember that he was still a small boy. His father sent him away for a few days. He was confused, upset; he didn't at all understand why he was being sent away. When he returned, he discovered that her wedding was in progress. His family had sent him away so that he would not be able to attend it.

"He thought he was in love. He wept when he realized he would never see her again. A nine-year-old child given away to a thirty-five-year-old man! That was her husband's age: thirty-five. It is criminal, but it's still happening. And people justify it by invoking the authority of Islam. I call it a crime against Islam. They were so young. Perhaps it wasn't love. Whatever it was, her loss marked him for life."

Tears have begun to appear in the corners of Mr. Sharifzadeh's eyes. A smile appears on Sheikh Nosrat's face. Mr. Sharifzadeh smiles embarrassedly and tries to wipe his eyes, "He does not talk about this and he has never married. After his father's death he left his village and somehow found his way to this place. You see what love can do to you?"

Howard whispers to his friend, "What caused you to tell me his story?"

Mr. Sharifzadeh struggles to compose himself. When he speaks, his voice is very low, and Howard has to strain to hear his words. "Because I feel that you are in love. And I don't want you to lose your love. You must pay attention. Life in Tabriz will go on without me, you, or our struggle. I suggest you ask the woman you love to marry you and go back to your home and live a fulfilling life. That would also be a gift from God."

Mr. Sharifzadeh prepares to leave. "It's late, my friend, and I must say goodnight. Remember my words, and do not let go of what you love."

Howard watches his friend walk slowly away into the night. The trees are heavy with snow. Howard walks home, kicking up little flurries of snow.

* * *

A beautiful sunset breaks over the mountains. It's a warm, vibrant day.

Helen walks outside to the yard to hang some wet clothes. She looks out and sees a male rider approaching in the distance. Dust rises from the ground. She continues to hang the rest of the clothes and watches the rider get closer and closer.

The unknown horseman is riding a black mare with precision and speed while holding the reins to a second black horse. He is wearing traditional tribal clothing and his face and head are covered. Helen's nervousness increases.

She takes her eyes off horse and rider for a moment. Then she senses movement behind a tree. A mild breeze moves the bedsheets back and forth as she pins them to the line. She knows someone is playing with her. She looks around for the man on the horse but he is nowhere in sight.

The clothesline begins to shake, slowly at first, then furiously.

Helen walks toward the house nervously.

The rider appears suddenly. He rides through the sheets, tossing them up into the wind, and shouting in a Turkish accent, "Helen? . . . Helen! . . . Helen!"

She is suddenly face-to-face with a freedom fighter holding a rifle. His face and head are covered. Shocked and frightened, she throws a wet cloth at him and runs away. Susan and Annie simultaneously run out of the house.

The horseman rides past Helen, yelling, "Hurry up! Get on the horse! We have to go."

Helen is covered with dust. The man turns and rides back towards her at full speed. He circles her, kicking up more dust and pointing at the horse he is leading by its reins. "Hurry up! Get on the horse! Helen, we have to go. Come on, Helen! It's okay. Get on the horse." Helen is terrified of horses. There had been an incident at her grandfather's house long ago.

She backs away from the horse, shouting, "What are you doing? Are you insane? I am American."

"I said, get on the horse! Don't you see you are mine? Hurry up and get on! We must go! Hurry up and get on!"

Helen yells back, "No! I am scared of horses! So just stop this nonsense, stop it! Stop it. I am American. I have nothing to do with your fight. I do not know what you want from me but you should leave now!"

Then several riders in traditional clothes appear from behind the trees, their faces covered.The main rider approaches Helen again and releases the reins he was holding. The horse trots towards Helen. She runs and the horse follows her. She falls to the ground and the horse jumps over her and runs away. She lies there scared, covered with dust and dirt.

After a second she is furious. She sits up and starts yelling furiously at the rider who was still riding around her in circles. "Crazy! Crazy madman! Go ahead and kill me! Run me over with a horse."

A man rides past her closely. She throws dirt at him. "Why are you doing this?" she screams. "You crazy excuse for a man!"

The rider retrieves the runaway horse and calms him down. He rides up to Helen and dismounts. Annie and Susan watch in fear while Helen sits in the dirt.

The rider is now very close to Helen. She flings a handful of dirt at him and kicks him in the groin. The rider falls to the ground.

Howard yells in pain: "God! You are violent." She turns back and approaches Howard as he pulls his scarf off.

"How dare you do this to me?" she shouts.

The rest of the men take their scarves off. Hajji Agha, Hossien Khan and a couple more of Howard's students stand there, grinning quietly. They begin to sing a traditional song. This is usually sung when a groom takes his bride away.

Howard sits beside Helen, stroking her forehead and brushing her dusty hair from her face. He takes his handkerchief from his pocket and wipes her tears away. "God. How beautiful you are. Just like a wild gypsy girl. As wild as the white horse."

"Why? Why did you do that?"

Howard just looks at her for a moment. The sunset highlights her skin. She looks just like a dusty angel.

"I wanted to catch you just like those wild horses. It must be done, the tradition that is custom around here."

"But I'm already yours; you caught me the day you walked into the yard."

"Do you trust me?"

"Yes, more than ever."

"Then get up on that horse. And prove your love for me."

Helen turns and looks at the horse standing close by. "Just like that?"

"Yes. It's the only way."

Suddenly a thought occurs to her. She grabs one of the damp scarves and wraps it around her head like a tribal female Iranian rider. Helen knows of the tradition. It requires the groom to steal his bride to prove his bravery. Then the woman consents to become his wife.

Helen walks over to the horse. She looks at the horse for a long time, and then glances back at Howard and her mother and sister. Howard reaches over and grabs her hand and gives her a boost. She is sitting on the horse, barely breathing and afraid to talk. But she is proving her love to Howard. It is the only way and she knows it. She turns toward Howard.

Howard mounts his horse and rides to her. Dismounting, he takes a silver necklace from his pocket and places it around her neck. The backdrop of colorful clothes lights up as the necklace sways gently in the breeze. They melt into each other's arms under the setting sun.

Howard turns to Annie and bows to her; he tips his hat.The two lovers ride into the hills, into the sunset. Helen feels like a weightless bird. The breeze flows through her hair and ruffles the horse's mane. She is no longer afraid. She is filled with love for Howard. Nothing else matters.

* * *

Mr. Wilson's family uses the church at the Memorial School for all kinds of occasions. A large crowd has gathered to celebrate Howard's engagement to Helen. The church is full of Americans and Iranians from all over Tabriz.

Howard had kissed Mr. Wilson's hand in delight when he, Mr. Wilson, had remarked that the two of them should get engaged.

The Reverend Vanneman reads a prayer as Howard puts the ring on Helen's finger. It is a short and beautiful ceremony. Wildflowers have been placed throughout the church. They glow against the stained-glass windows. After the ceremony, Mr. Wilson tells Helen and Howard, "Okay, now you two are on your own. I am proud and honored to have you in my family, Howard. Take care of each other."

Helen hugs her father then turns to her weeping mother. The church bell announces the end of the ceremony, and soon the church is empty.

Howard is sad that his parents are not with him. He misses his mother, particularly. His father is quiet and undemonstrative, a good husband and a responsible father but remote to his children. Howard misses his presence, too, but not as keenly as he does his mother's. He writes his mother regularly and inquires about his sisters. Every day he prays for them all. On his wedding night, he writes home with his news:

Dear Mother,

Amongst all the hardships we have had to endure, God has blessed me with one of his greatest gifts, my sweet Helen. Helen is my hope and love for the future. She reminds me of my dearest sisters whom I love with all my heart. At church, she always prays for you, for me, and for all the hungry and unfulfilled souls in the world. She is as tender-hearted as you and as playful as my dear sisters. Her warm, gentle wisdom washes over me like a spring rain. Each day I am with her, I am reborn.

* * *

The news of the engagement is soon known throughout the town.

Howard and Helen are awakened one morning by loud wedding music. Howard goes to the door. He remembers, sleepily, that the last time he had heard Iranian wedding music, he had made the acquaintance of the ferocious Shojaeh Nezam. Helen joins Howard in the doorway.

A large group, a including many of his students, is gathered outside the cottage. They have brought engagement presents: two horses, Persian rugs, lengths of brightly colored material, goats, sheep. A butcher is carrying half a skinned sheep on his shoulder. An older woman hands Helen a chicken. Hajji Agha gives Helen a jar containing pieces of silver and gold.

Several people begin to dance. The music grows louder.

The gathering demonstrates Howard's complete acceptance among the people of the city. They have embraced him as one of their own. He had left the American enclave and walked into their lives. Howard had brought other Americans out of their own narrow world and encouraged them to mingle with the locals.

They all dance. And for a few hours, all their troubles seem far away, even slightly unreal. Helen is happiest of all. She knows she will never be the same again. Howard has changed her forever. He has shown her a world that she would never have been able to explore on her own. They are no longer in a foreign land; Tabriz has become home.

But Howard's deepening friendship with Mr. Sharifzadeh makes her uneasy. She wonders anxiously where it will lead them.

* * *

Very few students have come to class. Howard is wondering why – they are usually so regular – when a back-bencher speaks up, "They want to be here. But their parents are scared to let them leave the house."

"What about yours? Aren't they scared?"

A different student answers, "My father thinks I will be safer here than in the streets."

Howard looks over the almost-empty room. "I cannot give a class with just a couple of students."

The boys stare at Howard for a moment to see if he is serious or joking, then one by one they leave the classroom. He watches them make their way down the street and disappear out of sight. He eventually gets up and walks into the hallway; it is silent. Only a few American teachers are about, and very few students. Howard walks out into the schoolyard, deeply preoccupied.

He sees neither Mr. Wilson nor the knot of American teachers who are all watching him.

Mr. Wright is among them. He has disapproved of Howard from the beginning. But now, many others have reservations about Howard's growing involvement in local affairs. Wright tells Mr. Wilson, "He's a bomb ready to explode. You must talk to him." But Mr. Wilson is not about to interfere in Howard's personal life. He strongly believes that a man's life is his own.

Loud sounds of disturbance are heard from the street. Howard walks very fast in that direction. The street is packed with small groups of people who are carrying rifles on their shoulders. He follows a large chanting group as they walk down the street. Shop owners begin to close their stores one by one; within an hour, the whole city is shut down, even the bazaars. Soon, every available bit of street is packed with people. Howard looks around for familiar faces. He reaches a square. A public meeting is in progress. Because the square is so full, people are perched in the trees just to watch the speakers as they prepare to address the mob. Howard jams himself into a small space on a crowded platform to get a better view.

The speaker is Mr. Sharifzadeh. He is being held up in the air. Mr. Sharifzadeh was blazing away in Turkish and Howard hears his words without understanding. Armed men punctuate his speech by raising their rifles. Mr. Sahrifzadeh is very convincing in the role of revolutionary orator. His audience grows more inflamed with every word he utters. Howard is thrilled at his transformation from the shy, quiet, sensitive scholar he knew and loved into this fire-breathing radical. He thinks of Thomas Paine, of Patrick Henry.

His speech over, Mr. Sharifzadeh is carried by his supporters through the dense mass of people. Somehow, Howard makes his presence known to his friend. Over the heads of the crowd, they shout at each other, but neither can make out what the other is saying.

Standing within the crowd, Howard wonders what he is doing there. He feels alone and empty. He wonders why he feels alone among so many people. And he wonders what he, an American, is doing among them. They have a cause, reason to be angry, reason to be inflamed. He feels lost, far away.

He senses someone's gaze upon him. A little boy is looking at him wonderingly. He smiles at Howard. He is staring at the little boy when, suddenly, he is carried away by the surging mass of people. He turns and tries to look for the little boy. But he has vanished.

The crowd reaches an old, dilapidated building. It is known to locals as the "Tabriz drill."

The revolutionaries in Tabriz

Inside, the place is packed. In every corner, a speaker is addressing a group of people. Many are carrying rifles. There are men and boys whose ages range from ten to eighty. Men, women, and children across the room are making donations of jewelry, money, blankets, etc.

Howard sees a man named Ali Musio. He has met Ali Musio at

Mr. Sharifzadeh's house. A fighter, a revolutionary, a simple man with passionate loyalties. Howard moves towards him but Ali Musio is in a hurry. He leaves with his men before Howard can reach him.

Howard is wandering around the room when he feels a hand on his shoulder.

He turns around to see Hajji Agha. "Hello, sir."

Howard is delighted. "Hajji Agha! It is so good to see you! Tell me, tell me. What's going on?"

Hajji Agha's voice goes somber. "Mohamme

ad Ali Shah is preparing to attack the Parliament and close it down. Several clergymen have gone over to his side. They are led by Sheikh Fazlolah Nory. They want to take our remaining freedoms away from us. We can't let that happen. We cannot allow another dictatorship. The people of Tabriz have risen against him, and the Tabriz assembly has voted to oust the shah from his throne. They say his actions are against the constitution. It was Mr. Sharifzadeh who announced the news to our people."

Howard follows the crowd into the drill in Tabriz. He looks at the people thronging the drill. "They are registering to go to Tehran to defend the Parliament. We have sent a telegram to every city in Iran about the assembly's decision."

Howard looks around at the men wearing mismatched outfits; some don't even know how to hold a rifle. Men are wearing several hats in different colors. The wearing of hats is customary here. A person's hat tells a great deal: his social status, his provenance.

"Who's going to lead them?"

Before Hajji Agha can reply, the crowd bursts into loud cheers.

A man of medium build enters, mounted on a palomino horse.

He is followed by two more mounted men. He wears a traditional hat and carries a rifle; several ammunition belts are slung across his shoulder. He is welcomed with thunderous applause and sustained cheering.

"Who's that man?"

"Sattar Khan. But he goes by Sardar. The national leader." There is no mistaking the deep pride with which these words are spoken.

Sattar Khan (Sardar)

Sardar and his son

"And that is Bagher Khan."

Another well-armed mounted warrior rides into the courtyard. He is received with the same warmth.

Bagher Khan

To Howard, both Sattar Khan and Bagher Khan look like ordinary men who haven't had any formal military training. An old woman loses her balance and falls on him. He helps her to her feet and she walks her over to the donation box. With a shaky hand, she drops a few coins and some old jewelry into the box. Someone helps the elderly woman away; she looks back gratefully at Howard.

A man, a Westerner by his appearance, enters and begins taking pictures. Howard walks to the donation box and drops in all the money he has. He stands there for a moment; then he takes his watch off and drops it into the box. His hand is shaken by many people; he is embraced and kissed. Sattar Khan has been watching Howard. Very deliberately, he salutes Howard, never taking his eyes off the American's eyes, looking deeply into them.

The photographer, an Irish reporter for the Herald newspaper, joins Howard and Hajji Agha.

"Moore," he says, holding out his hand. "I write for the papers."

"Baskerville," Howard says, shaking hands. "Howard Baskerville."

"You sound American."

"I am."

"Irish, myself. What paper are you on?"

"I am not. I teach history at the Mission School."

"Very good! I write it and you teach it." Moore says. "I wonder how a few hundred men, with no formal training and no equipment, expect to ride into Tehran and defeat the well-equipped and trained soldiers of the shah. You seem to have an idea. I saw you make a donation."

Before Howard can answer the question, Hajji Agha interrupts smilingly. "Do you believe in faith, Mr. Moore?"

And Howard adds, "They have faith. Many of them don't even know how to fire a rifle. But their hearts are full of faith, and that can be more valuable than any formal training in the world."

"What these men need are training and organization more than faith and donations." And with that deflating remark, Moore takes his leave. Howard decides that he does not like the man very much.

Bagher Khan (left) and Sardar (right) with their revolutionary men

Yepren Khan, an Armenian activist, and Sardar Bahador, who were with Sardar

Yepren Khan, an Armeninan activist, and Jafar Gholykhan Bkhatiary, who were with Sardar

* * *

Dawn in Tabriz. There is just enough light to see one's way around. Howard walks through a quiet alley listening to the stray cats converse about their hard lives.

Howard walks past the bakery. It opens earlier than the other shops. The oven has to be heated and the bread cooking by sunrise, because soon customers will be coming in for their morning loaves. It takes a couple of hours to make the dough and cook the fresh bread, so a few workers show up fairly early. Howard waves to one. The man shouts that his hot bread is ready. One of the other workers comes out to see if Howard is coming in. He shouts in Farsi, "Greetings, Mr. Howard. What time will you be back?" Howard replies in careful broken Farsi, "After the *hamoom*. I come after *hamoom*."

The man laughs, "Good, Mr. Howard, good!"

An alley in Tabriz

* * *

By *hamoom*, Howard meant the public bathhouse. There were just a few covered bathhouses in Tabriz in those days. The most famous was the Hajji Ghafar bathhouse. Mr. Sharifzadeh patronized it; he was a friend of the owner, Hajji Ghafar. Howard had read about Iranian bathhouses and the massages that were given in them. When he told Mr. Sharifzadeh about his interest in the bathhouse, Mr. Sharifzadeh invited him to Hajji Ghafar's at once.

After that, he visits the bathhouse every week. He likes to watch the people, the chanting of the masseurs, the hot pool, the freezing-cold pool. He is constantly trying to encourage other Americans to visit Hajji Ghafar's. But no one else is interested. He tells Helen that the bathhouse has some kind of magic; it really takes away one's tiredness and lifts the soul. It cleanses physically and mentally.

At Hajji Ghafar's there is a large pool in the middle with freezing-cold water that chills to the bone. After leaving the steamy hot main pool, one enters the cold one immediately. The ceiling is high, twenty to thirty feet. There are four-foot fabric-covered stands around the pool for people to sit on. They leave their clothes and belongings inside the tall lockers that line the back room. If it is a busy day, Thursday or Friday, and no lockers are available, then most will leave their belongings on the floor.

Everything inside the bathhouse is made from solid soft stone. At the entrance, workers hand out a couple of towels and a piece of material called a *loung*. The *loung* is wrapped around the waist; the towel goes over the shoulder. There is a place where you can lie down for a while, if one wants to, after the bath. Hajji Ghafar's also has a tea house.

Before entering the main part of the bathhouse, bathers must wash their feet in a small pool.

When Howard enters the bathhouse, he is free of all his worries. When the situation in Tabriz is especially bad, he stays in the bathhouse until his low spirits have passed. He always walks out refreshed, feeling almost a new man.

* * *

Howard reaches Hajji Ghafar's. Leaning against a wall, Hajji Agha is waiting for him. A worker brings towels and an extra red *loung* for Howard. The *loung* can be used as a towel as well. The *lounges* are always red. Whenever he visits, Howard is given extra towels and a new *loung* because he is an esteemed patron and a generous tipper. Howard and Hajji Agha cover themselves and make their way to the cold pool. They dangle their feet in the cold water and await Mr. Sharifzadeh's arrival.

It is still very early, and the bathhouse is quiet. As other customers begin to arrive, they see Howard and stop to shake his hand and chat. Soon, the place is almost full. A man serves tea to Howard and Hajji Agha. Mr. Sharifzadeh arrives. Everyone rises and utters a prayer for him. He goes up to Hajji Ghafar and takes a seat; a man serves him tea.

After his preparations are complete, Mr. Sharifzadeh calls to Howard and Hajji Agha. "In the name of God. Let's go." They enter the main bathhouse to the sound of people chanting prayers; the sound echoes through all the rooms in the bathhouse.

Steam has filled the whole room. Men lean on the soft-stoned rock benches and pray. The entire floor is covered by the same soft stone. There is a place where one can get tattoos and have one's skin waxed. Also, there are huge pieces of soft stone, six to eight feet long, in the area where massages are given. This is the section of the bathhouse that Howard loves the most. They walk through an archway and enter the hot pool; it is ten to twelve yards long and twenty feet deep. The steam makes it hard to see more than four feet in front of them. Howard and Hajji Agha go as early as possible so they can play in the pool. Playing is not allowed in the hot bath, but if no one is around, they indulge themselves.

Heat rises in the bathhouse; the place is filling up. Workers, masseurs, and tattoo artists begin to arrive. The three of them hold hands and Mr. Sharifzadeh says a prayer for them.

From the main part of the bathhouse comes the sound of someone singing. It is Mashty Kazem chanting while giving a massage. Mashty Kazem has been working at the bathhouse for forty years. He has a powerful voice, and Howard always asks for him. Howard turns to Mr. Sharifzadeh but can barely make him out in the steamy atmosphere. The first time he saw Mr. Sharifzadeh, Howard was reminded of the blind drummer boy. He cannot explain this to himself. Now, he looks closer, and seems to see the blind boy before him. He moves a little closer, only to see Mr. Sharifzadeh surface. Howard is bewildered. His face shows his confusion.

It is too hot to stay in the bath. They get out, walk to the stands, and await their turn to be washed. Howard watches several workers washing the men one by one. They work as a team. One scrubs the customer with soap and a scrubber, while another brings hot water from the pool and washes the soap off. On the other side, some men are getting massages. Two men are getting tattoos. Mr. Sharifzadeh does not approve of tattoos. But he believes that people should be free to do as they please, provided they do no harm to others. A tattoo is a badge of courage and honor. The bigger the tattoo, the stronger the wearer supposedly is. All the designs are taken from Persian literature and mythology.

Three workers approach them and begin to soap and scrub them. A young boy pours water on them. They wait for their massages. This is Howard's favorite bathhouse ritual. Mashty Kazem likes and respects Howard and makes sure that Howard is happy when he walks out of the bathhouse.

Hajji Agha won't let himself be massaged. That could be painful. And he couldn't bear the weight of strong men exerting so much force on his back and neck. When masseurs get hold of a young boys like Hajji Agha, they are merciless. They delight in testing their endurance. So Hajji Agha is content to sit and watch and listen. Howard wonders how an illiterate old man like Mashty Kazem can sing so captivatingly. He does not understand a word, but the singing still transports him. He has come to believe that Persian bathhouses are filled with a mystical energy.

Howard has a deep admiration for Persian culture, for philosophers like Omar Khayyam, Hafez, Saddi, Sheikh Abosaeed Aboulkher, Abou Ali Senna, for Rumi and Shams. He has read that it was Shams who influenced Rumi. In fact, Rumi found his path after talking to Shams. Actually, each fostered the other's development. They had shown each other the light and the darkness and the world that connected each to the other. Mashty Kazem puts Howard in mind of Rumi or Shams.

Hajji Agha watches Howard go limp with the massage and the chanting. Howard has told him that sometimes during his massages, he becomes so relaxed that he loses consciousness. Howard can barely open his eyes. He glances over at Mr. Sharifzadeh, about five feet away. He looks at Hajji Agha for a second and falls asleep.

He has a dream, perhaps even a vision. A curtain opens in the steam and a man appears. He is shaking a piece of red material. The steam rises from the material. Then, a lion, ready to spring, appears in the steam. A wise old man, wearing a long, loose, green outfit, appears out of the steam and holds out his hand to Howard. Happily, Howard reaches for it, and falls to the ground, just as Mashty finishes his massage and walks away, still chanting.

Howard hits his head hard on the rock. Hajji Agha is beside him instantly, calling for help. Mr. Sharifzadeh rushes up. Mashty Kazem goes on chanting, oblivious of the clamor. Hajji Agha and Mr. Sharifzadeh carry Howard out of the bathhouse and set him down on the grass. They splash him with ice-cold water.

Mashty Kazem then walks up and slaps the unconscious Howard hard across the face. Howard jumps up, slightly opening his eyes. Mashty calls for a bowl of water and honey. Howard drinks the mixture and recovers. Hajji Agha watches Mashty walk coolly away.

Hajji Agha and Mr. Sharifzadeh help Howard put his clothes back on. The arrival of the school carriage is announced.

Someone had sent a messenger to Helen. She is waiting anxiously by the carriage. "What has happened, Hajji Agha?" They send for a doctor who examines Howard and pronounces him all right but in need of rest.

Mr. Sharifzadeh sees that Hajji Agha is terribly shaken. He puts an around Hajji Agha's shoulders. "Hajji Agha, he will be okay. Go home and relax." Mr. Sharifzadeh watches to make sure Hajji Agha heads toward his home.

* * *

Howard sits by the window drinking tea and gazing at the mountains above Tabriz. He is covered in thick blankets and a scarf. He hasn't recovered all his strength yet. The town is covered in snow. The mountains look like a beautiful giant ark. Helen comes in and sits beside him. She, too, contemplates the mountains.

"Does someone live up there?" Howard becomes aware of her presence. "It seems like it." Helen continues, "Moses, Mohammad, and Jesus always would go to the mountains to talk to God. When I was a little girl, I thought that was where He lived." Howard takes Helen's hand and holds it tightly, "He does. But here there is also some kind of spirit that follows you everywhere."

Howard lies on his bed in the middle of the night; his eyes are shut, but he is wide awake. He is tormented by the same recurring question: What should he do? He has become two different men; he is divided down the middle between his new life and his old one. This isn't his country. This isn't his struggle. He can go home if he wants to. There is plenty of good work to be done at home.

But, but, but. Mr. Sharifzadeh and Hajji Agha: they would die for him, he knows that. They are full of such passion. They are just men but they have great dreams. Merely men, yes, but men ennobled by their cause.

Perhaps he could write a book about the people and their struggle here. That, too, is a noble task. He could write articles and send them to the papers at home. Something might come of it. But no, nothing would. It is all too far away.

This is not your problem! Sooner or later, guests always leave, and you are a guest!

He wants to teach. He is a man of principle and integrity. He must follow his own path. He thinks of Jesus and is awakened to a pitch of feverish excitement. He almost cries out in passion. Jesus was full of love. He embraced all those around him. He let himself be hammered to a cross. He understood man's greatest flaws.

Amidst such thoughts Howard falls asleep.

* * *

The situation on the streets has worsened. If any stores open at all, it is just for an hour or two; then they quickly lock everything up again. Crowds of people are outside the telegraph office. They want news of Tehran. There is always a group waiting for news.

Howard and Helen wait with the group Mr. Moore emerges from the telegraph office in a great hurry. He pushes through the crowd and, catching sight of Howard, shouts, "Telegrams are coming in from all over the country. The whole country seems to have risen up against the shah. People in the cities of Saveh and Gazvin have started to make their way toward Tehran to help fight the government forces."

Howard shouts back, "And here? What about here?"

"Sardar and Bagher Khan are leaving for Tehran with their men. I have to get to the other side. Goodbye! For God's sake, take care of yourselves."

Chapter Five
The Calm Before the Storm

A kind of calm settles on Tabriz. The stores begin to stay open longer, and people appear on the streets. Snow is still falling, blanketing everything.

Howard and Helen are absorbed in each other. And, one day, the sounds of gunfire return.

Howard is restless and anxious. Helen is too, but all her anxieties are concentrated on Howard.

The situation in the city changes. Panic grips the citizens. The ruthless Shojaeh Nezam is rumored to be on his way. A group gathers at the governor's office, asking for help. The governor assures them there is nothing to worry about and that the necessary steps have been taken to secure their safety. But it was clear that nothing had been done.

Mir Hashem and Mirza Hassan Mojahed, two clergymen, accompanied by several other clergymen, begin to walk the streets asking people to revolt against the governor and others like him who really only do the shah's bidding But the people need no convincing; they already know the situation.

Mir Hashem with his followers who support warlords and the shah

Mir Hashem with Zargam and Amir Arshad

The National Council soon realizes that the shah is trying to take Tabriz while it is most vulnerable. Shojaeh Nezam's arrival is timed to coincide with the absence of Sardar and Bagher Khan, while they were still in Tehran. The National Council immediately sent them a message to return.

On their return, Sardar and Bagher Khan organize their men into groups. Each group consists of twenty-five men; one man is put in charge. The leaders of each group communicate with Sardar or Bagher Khan for orders. They divide the city between them. Bagher Khan and his men were responsible for defending the streets and the bazaars, while Sardar and his men are responsible for defending Amirkhiz and the National Council. The city nervously awaits further developments.

Then several clergymen, led by the treacherous Mirza Hassan Mojtahed, defect to the shah and the Russians. They start an Islamic assembly and a paper called *Molah Amoo*. They begin to condemn the National Council, calling it illegal and against Islamic principles. They target Sardar, Mr. Sharifzadeh, Bagher Khan, and others, accusing them of atheism _ an offense, according to Islamic law, punishable by death. A few days later, they gather men from the cities of Doochy and Sorkhab and proceed to loot houses and stores throughout Tabriz.

The situation is complicated by the disunity among the cities in the country. Several cities dislike one another. They are not bound together by any cause. Amirkhyz fights for liberty and freedom like Tabriz, while Doochy and Sorkhab support the shah. People begin saying that Shojaeh Nezam is not the only warlord headed toward the city; other groups are on their way as well. Rahim Khan, Sama Khan, Zargham Khan, and Faramarz Khan are rumored to be entering the city soon with their men. Everyone rushes to gather supplies, while some flee Tabriz with their families. The city looks desolate.

The National Council of Tabriz is organized by individual citizens. The government has nothing to do with it. In official eyes, it is an illegal organization.

The first meeting of the National Council is held. At first, no one knows it exists; its members always meet in secret. But the Council's membership grows, and soon their meetings can no longer be secret.

Rahim Khan, a ruthless warlord

* * *

It is Aideh Ghorban, a Muslim holiday. The school is closed. Howard makes his way through deserted streets to Mr. Sharifzadeh's house.

Mr. Sharifzadeh is in a private meeting with some of his friends. They are startled to see Howard, but Mr. Sharifzadeh reassures them that Howard can be trusted, and the men relax. Ali Musio enters shortly after and greets Howard; he asks for Mr. Sharifzadeh. Mr. Sharifzadeh asks Howard to wait for him.

Howard goes to another room in the house. After some time, he becomes restless. There is a knock on the door. Mr. Sharifzadeh's helper is nowhere to be seen. Howard hesitantly opens the door. A tall woman, completely veiled, stands there holding a bowl in her hand.

Howard says, "I am a guest here."

The lady hands him the bowl. She says, *aush*, and nothing else. Then she turns and walks away.

There are many different kinds of *aush* dishes, made with wheat, chicken, noodles, and beans. Not knowing what to think, Howard stands rooted to the spot. When the helper finally appears, Howard hands him the bowl.

Howard walks out of the yard and into the street. All the stores have been closed for some time. Howard peers into his favorite herb shop; it is pitch-black and empty. He notices a group of suspicious-looking armed men on the other side of a small stream. They are scattered along the bank; they seem to be carrying out some sort of inspection. Howard approaches the bridge.

Just then, Hajji Agha arrives with a couple of his friends. They, too, are interested in what the suspicious-looking men are doing.

Hajji Agha runs towards Howard. "No, no, no. Please don't, sir! Not now. Those are Shojaeh Nezam's men."

"What are they doing here?"

Hajji Agha coaxes Howard off the bridge before he attracts the armed men's attention. He speaks quickly. "They have come to join the clergy who oppose the movement. And they support the shah and the Russians." Tugging gently but determinedly at Howard, Hajji Agha continues nervously. "There is a rumor that the shah has been forced to sign a peace agreement with the Iranian Parliament. He cannot publicly send a force to fight Sardar. So now, he has hired thieves, murderers, and disloyal clergymen."

Howard has been doggedly resisting Hajji Agha's efforts to drag him away from the bridge.

"They are a vicious organized gang, Howard. They have been sent here to destroy us all. They will not hesitate to shoot you on sight, especially you, because you got away last time."

Howard stares down the length of the bridge, "Then I have to hear their side of the story for myself. Hajji Agha, I have altered my profession; I am now a reporter and a historian."

Helplessly, Hajji Agha follows his teacher. Soon, they are in an armed camp. They pass Shojaeh Nezam's men, a mixture of Lores, Turks, and Kurds, each armed with a rifle and ammunition belts. They are watched closely as they make their way to the heart of the Islamic assembly, the headquarters for the opposition to the freedom movement.

Hajji Agha pleads with Howard to turn back.

"Calm down, Hajji Agha. Nothing is going to happen."

They enter a large yard, packed with armed men. They see Mirza Hassan Mojtahed standing in a second-story window. He is addressing a crowd in Turkish. Standing beside him is Shojaeh Nezam.

"Men," he declares, "we are happy to see our friend Shojaeh Nezam here to help support us against a group of atheists. What the National Council, Sardar, and his followers want is against God's will. It's against Islam. We have to send them to hell, and we must support our king!"

One of Shojaeh Nezam's men recognizes Hajji Agha and Howard. He makes a threatening move in their direction. Shielding Hajji Agha all the while, Howard pushes him away. They are immediately surrounded. Raised rifles are aimed at the pair.

A single shot rings out. Shojaeh Nezam holds his rifle up.

Howard speaks loudly to Hajji Agha; he keeps an eye on Shojaeh Nezam. "Tell them I am a reporter for the American newspaper and you work for me."

Shojaeh Nezam and the others look doubtful.

Howards says, "Tell them I am here to hear their side. They must tell the world where they stand and their motivations for fighting."

Mirza Hassan Mojtahed screams in Turkish, "Tell him he is not welcome here!"

The men close in on Howard and Hajji Agha, but Shojaeh Nezam shouts out. as he fires into the air again, "Tell him I do not like him, and his presence here is an insult. He owes his life and yours to Mirza Hassan . . . this will be the last time I let him leave my presence alive!"

He yells out an order: "Let them go. Move back." He fires twice more into the air. A narrow passage is created and Howard and Hajji Agha make their way out of the yard. Howard holds Hajji Agha's arm tightly.

Several men, their faces partially covered, emerge from various directions. They appear to be escorting Howard and Hajji Agha from the armed camp. They are joined by others and, all together, they lead Howard and Hajji Agha across the bridge to safety.

The men had been sent by Mr. Sharifzadeh and Ali Musio. Mr. Sharifzadeh and Ali Musio reach the two men shortly afterward.

"My friend," says Mr. Sharifzadeh, "I did not mean to ignore you. A pressing matter required my attention. Once I realized you were missing, I looked for you and tracked you to this bridge. You should not have taken that kind of risk."

"Why did they risk themselves to help me?"

"Because you are our guest. Because you are a friend. Because you were sent to us by God."

Ali Musio mounts his horse and rides away. Mr. Sharifzadeh

turns to Howard once again, "A conspiracy is in progress."

"How are you going to protect the city?"

"You already know the answer to your question. When you compare our weapons and experience with that of our enemy, perhaps you are seized by doubts. But we will protect the city. The people will fight."

Howard says nothing but wonders if the people really can win or if Mr. Sharifzadeh will fail his people.

* * *

Sardar and Bagher Khan have been busy with their preparations. They have built so many foxholes throughout the city that one cannot walk down the street without seeing one on every corner. The city is waiting to be set on fire. Young boys randomly play in the streets, ducking and diving from foxhole to foxhole. Their parents soon hurry them back indoors.

* * *

At the school, Howard doesn't know what to do. Many students do not show up because they are worried that fighting will break out at any time. Their parents will not let them out of the house. Howard's students are from the richest families, the elite of Tabriz. They have plenty of money and food, and are receiving the best education. They have no reason to fight other than because of their conscience and their love for their city. Their parents are terrified that they will get involved.

Howard's students are absolutely still. Finally, he says, "Perhaps today we should talk about liberty."

The school bell rings unexpectedly. Everyone knows the battle has begun. The students rush out of the classroom. Howard walks into the hallway. The bell continues to ring. Mr. Wilson stands at the end of the hall, shouting at the students to go straight home.

All the students have left except Hajji Agha. He is smoking a cigarette. He wants to tell Howard to go home; he does not have to worry, the Americans will be left alone. This is not his problem; it's not his war. He knows Howard should go home, but a part of him wants him to stay. Howard's presence gives all of them – Hajji Agha and his classmates – hope, energy, and courage. They want to defend their city, their families, and the people's right to freedom. But their rich, powerful fathers will not permit them to join Mr. Sharifzadeh and his friends.

Their fathers believe they have everything; there is no reason for them to fight. But far more than personal security and luxurious living is at stake. To live with honor means follow your principles; and by ignoring the cries in the street, their spirits are being killed. Howard could draw the best out of them. Hajji Agha knows this. He takes one last look at Howard before rushing away.

Later Howard finds Hajji Agha standing alone on a street corner. They walk, without any idea where their feet are leading them. Suddenly they find themselves in the thick of the fighting. Riding toward them from the distance is Hussein Khan. He sounds frantic. "Sardar is in danger! The enemy has dug several holes through his neighbor's house. They are closing in on him; we have to defend him."

Hajji Agha is overwhelmed by warmth for Hussein Khan; student just like him, armed and mounted. He is very proud of

Hussein Khan. He is ashamed of himself; he should be doing the same. He wants to be brave and help, but his father will not allow it. In fact, his father is probably looking for him now.

Howard and Hajji Agha come up to the end of a street. They see a couple of students running toward Sardar's house. They call out to others to join them. Hajji Agha and Howard join them.

It does not take them long to get there. As they near Sardar's house, the fighting intensified. Sardar's house is at the heart of it. All the fighting forces throughout the city head for Sardar's house. It is as if a war were raging in every backyard. People hide in their houses.

Sardar's men waiting for the enemy

Hajji Agha is paying more attention to Howard than to the fighting. He is waiting for Howard's next move. Howard's safety is foremost in his thoughts; he would never forgive himself if something were to happen to Howard.

The enemy is about to reach Sardar's house. Veiled women reload the freedom fighters' guns. Howard knows Hajji Agha wants to help. He knows he is afraid of his father. Then he sees Sardar leaping from roof to roof. He is fired at and he returns fire, killing several men. A bullet strikes his hand. Sardar must stay alive, and they all know it. He is the heart of the people; he keeps alive their will to fight.

Ignoring his wound, Sardar continues to fight. He will not hide from the battle and watch as his men die; he will face the danger with them. Moore takes cover and sets up his photographic equipment.

Howard runs forward, staying close to the side of the building, and Hajji Agha follows. Debris falls all around them, and bullets fly over their heads. They take cover behind a broken wall and see a group of the warlord's men, shooting wildly, advance steadily on Sardar's troops. As Howard watches, a goat wanders into the middle of the fighting and is shot dead by the warlord's men. A frail old man walks calmly to the goat, picks it up and walks away. When he passes Howard, he turns and says:

I was told, as I find my being,
I will be judged and punished
For all my sins
Look at me
I am aged, tired, bored of being
Still keep doing sin after sin
Yet no power has stopped me
Then I wonder
Where is the justice I was told
Would come up on me?

An armed freedom fighter falls from the roof and lands beside Howard. His rifle falls at Howard's feet. Helplessly, Howard and Hajji Agha watch the life ebb out of him.

Then Ali Musio and his men arrive. Ali Musio had been busy defending the bazaars, but had quickly rushed over to help when he learned how pressed Sardar's troops were. His men were under intense fire as they rode across the river. Some fell along the way. But now Ali Musio's men are in the thick of the fighting. Hajji Agha watches the warlord's men drop from the rooftops, one by one. Someone is shooting, but no one can tell who it is in the chaos.

He turns to Howard but does not see him anywhere. He notices that the dead man's rifle is missing. He sees a house that has been demolished by a cannon on the other side and begins to walk over cautiously. He is still trying to find the source of the bullets when three more men drop from the rooftop. Ali Musio and his men have surprised the enemy from behind and are now distracting them as Sardar and his men gain some ground. Hajji Agha can no longer stand around and watch; he runs through the street grabbing ammunition belts from dead bodies and runs back toward the damaged house. Suddenly he recognizes Howard's head through the rubble; he is aiming and shooting down the enemy faster than Hajji Agha can blink. He cannot believe his eyes: Howard is the mystery shooter! He runs up to him and hands him the ammunition belts. Howard reloads his rifle, adjusts his position, and shoots again, dropping a few more soldiers. Hajji Agha is surprised at how focused Howard is. Hajji Agha is slightly startled by the lack of expression on Howard's face.

Hajji Agha sees Sardar staring at Howard. He seems to acknowledge Howard with a fleeting gesture. Then he continues to fight his way through the crowd. Sardar and Ali Musio's forces finally meet amongst the surrendering enemy forces. The freedom fighters surround Sardar, cheering in victory. The crowd of unarmed watchers is ecstatic.

The people of Tabriz do not know that the shah has already bombed the Parliament and arrested all the representatives while the fighting was going on. They also do not know that Tabriz was the last city left for the shah and his accomplices to conquer. Had the Tabriz fighters lost this first attack, it would have been the end of the movement.

By some miracle, Tabriz survived. The fighters know that had the enemy succeeded, the movement would have collapsed. And the area of Amirkhyz would have been looted and burned and the women kidnapped or raped. There would have been nothing left to live for. But a few men, led by Sardar, had turned back the well-organized and well-equipped forces armed by the shah.

Hajji Agha was enjoying it so much that, for a moment, he forgot about Howard. In fact, if Mr. Moore had not appeared around the corner, he would not have remembered Howard was there. He turns and looks at Howard holding the rifle, then he looks as he places it on a broken wall. A young boy watches Howard. Their eyes lock for a bit. Then the young boy grabs the rifle and runs away. Howard begins to walk away. He cannot say a word to anyone. He will not talk to Mr. Moore, either. Mr. Moore smells a story. Hajji Agha is worried about Howard. He's impressed and shocked by his knowledge and skill in handling a rifle. Yet he knows how hard it would be for Howard to kill. Hajji Agha watches him wandering through the dead bodies and sits down on a crumbling wall.

Hospital room in Tabriz during the fighting

* * *

Hajji Agha rushes to the telegraph office. The office is packed with reporters. They are trying to send word to their offices. He sees Moore, the Irish reporter, yelling at the telegraph operator. He moves closer to him. He's practically screaming, "The fighting was very heavy today in Tabriz. The shah in Tehran had surprised everyone. He had Russian soldiers bomb the Parliament. The Parliament is destroyed. The forces also attacked Sardar's house. It is a life-and-death struggle for the leaders of the movement. Unless foreign help arrives, the city of Tabriz will fall. The whole nation has its eyes on Tabriz. If Tabriz is taken, the movement will be defeated. All hope of freedom will be gone."

Hajji Agha goes outside. There he learns more. The shah is under the thumbs of the Russians and the English. He does their bidding. Hajji Agha talks to several people he knows. Some of them once worked in the telegraph office and know his father. They used to come to his house for tea.

* * *

The gunfire has let up, and Hajji Agha finds himself at the Memorial School. He knocks on Howard's door. There is no answer. He runs toward the church.

The church is quiet. Hajji Agha rushes in and finds Howard kneeling before the statue of Christ. He is talking to it. The Reverend Vanneman stands beside him.

Howard whispers, "I have never killed anyone before. Why did I pick up the rifle and start shooting? I feel neither guilt nor remorse. I don't feel anything. I am celebrating their victory. How can one kill another human being and then celebrate? Does my grief arise only from not having helped earlier?"

Hajji Agha sees the sorrow on Howard's face. The Reverend

Vanneman is feels helpless.

Howard looks at the Reverend Vanneman for a moment and says, "I guess I am here for your help; I am lost."

Howard looks at the floor, then at Christ's statue, and then at the Reverend Vanneman. He gets to his feet and walks out of the church. Hajji Agha is waiting for him. There are tears in his eyes. Wordlessly, he pulls a telegram out of his pocket and hands it to Howard. Howard looks at it.

"They attacked the Parliament in Tehran at the same time they attacked Tabriz."

Howard returns the telegram to Hajji Agha. "I can't read Farsi yet."

* * *

The days go by. The fighting is sporadic. Neither side can establish a decisive advantage. Howard is wracked with guilt. He knows that he ought to feel remorseful for taking up arms, shooting at other men, even, perhaps, killing some. But he knows, equally, that the cause was just. He had helped defend Sattar Khan. And yet, were these the actions of a Christian? Could anything justify the taking of life? He was haunted by questions like these.

He has become friendly with Moore. The reporter takes him deep into the world of the armed struggle. They are in an opium den one night. Opium is one of Moore's weaknesses.

A man tells Howard and Moore, "You help my people. Train them. Give them guns. And I give you as much as you want."

"Jolly good," says Moore.

Howard looks disgusted.

Moore inhales deeply, "Don't give yourself airs, Baskerville." He points to a young man – Irish? English? Howard cannot say. "I know how you feel. But that one there has seen much worse. Just back from Tehran. Ask him."

Hearing English speech, the young man, whose name is Robert, edges up to them. "I was there," he whispers. "I saw the whole thing. God! And I was on my way to the station to catch the carriage to Tabriz."

* * *

It was too quiet. I could hear horses moving about. But I didn't see them. Then I heard men, but they were quieter, didn't see them at first, either. A troop of Russians, cavalry and foot soldiers, appeared. I was on my way to the square in front of the Parliament. It was happening. I had heard that there might be trouble. I was very nervous.

I saw men, locals by the look of them, taking up positions on the roof of the Parliament. Men on the buildings around the Parliament, too. It was getting light. I wished I had someone who spoke English with me. Two tea houses were open, probably for breakfast. There were a few people inside. But the tea houses were shutting up. They were in a terrific hurry. I got inside one just before they banged the shutters down.

I saw a carriage enter the square. By the look of it, there was someone important inside. I heard a voice come from the carriage. An order, probably. The carriage left the square.

A few minutes later, I saw four of those big Russian guns, "super guns," I suppose they are called, being rolled into the square. They were positioned in the middle of each street leading to the Parliament building.

Then, three Russian soldiers walked by the window of the tea house. They stopped and stared inside. A bad moment, I can tell you. I found a back door and got out of the tea house. There were Russians everywhere. I was looking for a place to hide when a door in the alley opened. A man whistled at me. He motioned me inside. I just avoided the group of Russians who had arrived in the alley.

The house belonged to someone very rich. I was told his name but I can't remember now. Luxurious. Lots of rooms. Art everywhere. And furniture and rugs. All sorts of things. The man's name was Jammal. The man who had whistled at me. He spoke very good English, this man.

"You must stay here," he said. "I'll tell you when it is safe to leave."

We went upstairs. Jammal turned his binoculars onto the square. I asked him what the Russians were doing in Tehran.

"Who else can the shah hire to do his dirty work?"

We watched the square. An old clergyman hobbled into the square. Two men were supporting him. They crossed the square and walked towards the Parliament. There was a crowd in the square. I'd say a thousand people. They were chanting. They moved towards the Russians. There were over a hundred of them, I'd say. You must remember that there are two Russians to each "super gun," so there were fewer than a hundred Russians to fight this big crowd. The Russians surrounded the old clergyman, and the two men with him. They started beating them up. The old man fell down. Jammal and I were at quite a distance from this scene. But we saw the blood on the old man.

It puzzled me. I asked Jammal, "Why aren't they fighting the Russians? There are so many more of them. They could take over the guns."

Jammal said, "Perhaps they don't want to kill any Russians. That would give them a reason to invade places like Tabriz."

"But they are here."

"Unofficially. Unofficially. If you fought them, you would be inviting them to stay. Fighting them would make it official."

I saw the Mazro rifle on a shelf in the room.

In the square, the old clergyman was struggling to his feet. He could barely stand. Men rushed out of the Parliament. They flung themselves at the soldiers. Someone fired a shot. In the air, I think. Probably an order, because the battle got truly under way after that. The "super guns" opened fire on the Parliament. There was gunfire from the roof of the Parliament. The Russians returned fire. The crowd in the square scattered in every direction. Bodies dropped to the ground. Men, horses. A scene of pure carnage.

A shell hit our building. Jammal and I fell to the floor. When we returned to the window, we saw that the Russians were having the worst of it. They were retreating, but still blazing away.

A mounted Russian and others on foot entered the square. They were beaten back. This raised some weak cheers. But there were more "super guns" in the square now, and they were really blasting away at the Parliament. One of the shells, probably more than one, must have been particularly damaging, because the building simply crumbled.

We knew we had to leave the building. It was only a matter of time before we were found. We blindly ran out into the alley. Bodies, blood, people being beaten up, being shot: I saw all this. But it is all hazy now. I can't remember any faces. Even Jammal's. We must have lost each other somewhere, because I found myself alone. I found my way to the station. The carriage to Tabriz was, miraculously, still running. I took it.

* * *

Mr. Moore whispers to Howard, "I had news of this from Tehran. I saw you dropping those vermin, in front of Sardar's house, one by one. And I thought perhaps I might be of assistance. I asked to train some of their men. You know, they really need help. You would be of great help to them."

Howard looks mystified. "I am a teacher and studying to become a minister."

"Weren't you a soldier once?"

"I was in the Army," Howard says, "very briefly."

Mr. Moore puffs at his pipe, "Well, you can't claim to be a virgin or a nun, can you?"

* * *

The shah's men attack the city again. They are determined to finish Sardar and his men as soon as possible, perhaps within a few days. But it does not happen. The shah sends reinforcements. The attacking forces had been led to believe that Tabriz would fall easily. But they were wrong.

News of the Parliament bombing and the fall of Tehran has a lowers the spirits of the people. Many become despondent. They wonder who will come to their aid now. The wealthy classes are very worried; they have much to lose. And they are worried about retribution at the hands of the shah's men and, especially, the warlords' men.

Tabriz's National Council was organized mainly by highly influential politicians and the wealthy elite. They do nothing to help the people; eventually, it is dissolved. Two of the members of the National Council take sanctuary in the Russian consulate. Spirits in Tabriz are very low. Things look bleak. The fall of the city seems imminent.

Another assembly is organized by several activists. This is a mysterious organization. No one knows what it is called or who belongs to it. People call it "the invisible assembly." It is generally assumed that Sardar and Mr. Sharifzadeh are members. This organization takes over the responsibility of protecting the city and fighting for democracy. Despite the heavy fighting, which is continuous, and the odds against the freedom fighters, the city does not fall.

Howard is at home. The sounds of heavy fighting are all about him. He is anxious and feeling helpless. When night falls, restlessness drives him out of the house. His destination is Mr. Sharifzadeh's house.

He passes through deserted streets. Evidence of the fighting lies all around.

There is a meeting in progress at Mr. Sharifzadeh's. The "invisible assembly" is in session. Howard waits for the meeting to end.

Ali Musio comes in. He greets Howard with a weary smile and takes his place at the meeting. Anxiety and distress are written on every face. The discussion is passionate and carried on in Farsi and Turkish. Howard understands very little. How much longer can they hold out he wonders?

The meeting over, Mr. Sharifzadeh takes a place beside Howard.

"How is everything?" Howard asks, uselessly.

"As you can see, things are not going well."

"What do you hear from Teheran?"

"The worst news. The Parliament has been demolished."

"And what will happen to Tabriz?"

The question rouses Mr. Sharifzadeh. "Tabriz? Tabriz will fight!"

"Is it worth it? Just look at the odds."

"You know very well that it is, my dear friend. We cannot lose hope. God is with us."

"Hope!"

"Yes, hope. A man must hope until he is dead. Besides, we, too, have a great force of men behind us. Why should we not hope? Truth is on our side. There is power in truth."

"What men can you mean? The men hiding in their houses? The men who fled before the fighting began? Or the men sheltering in the Russian and English consulates?"

"All that you say is as it is. But when the time comes, they will all fight. They know, in their innermost hearts, what justice is. They will rise and defeat their enemies."

After a short pause, Mr. Sharifzadeh continues. "When a man's rights have been taken away from him, Howard, he will want them back. It takes longer in some cases. But eventually, he will get up and fight. It is in every man's nature to do so."

That night, Howard returns to his cottage from Mr. Sharifzadeh's looking even more preoccupied than usual. He is sitting at a table composing a letter to the American consul, Doty.

Helen watches him, worriedly. She is sympathetic to the struggle being waged by Mr. Sharifzadeh and his friends. But it is Howard whom she loves. And she is terrified that Howard will soon be so involved with Mr. Sharifzadeh and the others, and in the battle for Tabriz, as to be beyond her reach.

Howard looks up from the page. "My love, this is a list that I simply have to make up tonight. Go to bed. I won't be long."

"It isn't like you to remain neutral. You'll take sides. And what shall I do if you decide to join all of them?"

In bed Howard tosses and turns. He thinks scornfully of Doty. Neutrality, under the circumstances, isn't neutrality at all. Doty is hiding behind his profession. Howard doesn't believe he is neutral at all. Callous, heartless, indifferent. But not neutral.

To Doty, the people among whom he lives are not real. People like Doty inhabit their alien cocoons comfortably. Would he remain so diplomatically indifferent if he had seen, and heard, and smelled, and tasted this life as Howard had? Would his neutrality have survived a conversation with Mr. Sharifzadeh, or his speech? Could he remain neutral after enjoying the friendship and devotion of Hajji Agha?

Disconnected thoughts of tea houses, Mashty Kazem, hot bread, the sounds of chanting and prayer, Hajji Agha's voice saying, "No, Howard, no!" fill his mind. And he falls asleep.

* * *

He presents himself before the consul the next morning. They exchange pleasantries before Howard comes to the point.

"Mr. Doty, I came, really, to talk about the situation in Tabriz."

"The fighting, Mr. Baskerville?"

"Yes. That, too, but."

"Please don't make yourself anxious. All that is necessary has been done to ensure the safety of the Americans in Tabriz."

"I have no doubt that it has, Mr. Doty. But that isn't what."

"What else, Mr. Baskerville? What else could you want to ask me?"

"These people, Mr. Doty. I wonder if you realize that these people are not going to yield. I wonder if you realize that at all. They will fight to the death."

"Will they really? I wonder if they will."

"They will, most assuredly. They have faith, the will, and unshakeable convictions."

"Well, I wish them luck, Mr. Baskerville. I certainly hope they succeed."

"Hope, Mr. Doty? Hope isn't enough. They need our help."

"What exactly do you propose, Mr. Baskerville? That I write the President and ask for American soldiers to come here and take on the shah, the English, the Russians, and whoever else? Is that really what you suggest I do? You must be unfamiliar with our laws, Mr. Baskerville. Our laws, the Constitution of the United States, do not permit such meddling."

"I see. Yes. Does the Constitution then recommend that we watch passively as thousands of people are slaughtered? As they martyr themselves for the very American causes of individual liberty, justice, equality? Mr. Doty, let me tell you about Cyrus the Great, the Persian king. He was the most benevolent of men. In those faraway times, he proclaimed the equality of all faiths. When he conquered a city, he did not plunder it. He took nothing away from its people. He forgave his enemies, he rebuilt their cities. He brought just rule and fairness to people who had known only tyranny."

Mr. Doty gazes thoughtfully at Howard. "Mr. Baskerville, you are a passionate young idealist. I admire you for it, sir. I do very much. Would you permit me, as someone older, to offer you a word of advice? Your fervor is misplaced. This isn't your country. You are a guest here. You came here to earn a living. If you must serve a cause, go home. Leave this to them. Let their politicians sort it out among themselves."

"Mr. Doty, I did not come to Tabriz just to earn a living. I came to learn, among other things, how to become a better human being, a better Christian. The world is changing. Men in your profession ought to know that. We can't simply stand aside, pleading neutrality. We have to involve ourselves when the cause is just. It is an obligation, our moral duty, to help any people fighting to be free. That is what I think our Constitution urges us to do. And I think that is the highest of all American principles."

"I have done my duty, Mr. Baskerville," the consul says. "Before you leave, I must iterate my belief that you are a misguided young man. I warn you: The course you are taking is a dangerous one."

Chapter Six
Stalled Ambitions

The shah had expected Tabriz to fall at the same time as Tehran. But the bravery of Sardar, Bagher Khan, Ali Musio, and their men had thwarted him. All Persia's eyes are on Tabriz. Sattar Khan's name is known in every house in Iran. He is no longer just "Sattar Khan," Now, he is known simply as "Sardar," which means "national leader." The shah is sending more reinforcements. He has invited other warlords to Tabriz.

Rahim Khan is rumored to be on his way to Tabriz. One of the most powerful of the warlords, he is even more ruthless than Shojeah Nezam. The shah sends him a message, addressing him flatteringly as Sardar Nossrat. The shah asks him to finish off Sardar and capture the city of Tabriz. But Rahim Khan thinks a confrontation with the likes of Sardar is beneath him. Instead, he sends his son Buick Khan with seven hundred men. But Buick Khan is defeated by Bagher Khan.

After their defeat, Buick Khan and his men go to Baghmyshan, which is controlled by the shah's forces. They are warmly welcomed. But Buick Khan's men, enraged by their defeat, rampage through

Baghmyshan. In a few days of concentrated looting and pillage, they all but destroy Baghmyshan.

Rahim Khan is furious when he hears the news of his son's defeat. He arrives outside Tabriz and prepares to attack Bagher Khan and Sardar Khan. He wants the city to be looted and destroyed. He wants blood.

But the worst news for the people of Tabriz isn't the arrival of Rahim Khan. It is the Russian consul's declaration that the lives of Russian citizens in Tabriz are in jeopardy. He asks the shah for even more reinforcements. Now, rumors fly that the Russians are at the border poised to invade. Every Russian is told to hang a Russian flag outside his house. This is to preserve them from harm. Everyone who fears for his safety is told to hang a white Russian flag over his house. The consul also orders that a Russian flag be hung in the square. Neutrals and supporters of the shah are told to take refuge under the Russian flag.

More reinforcements are sent from Tehran, and Rahim Khan arrives: the noose begins to tighten around Sardar's forces. The pressure mounts. And Bagher Khan, who is responsible for guarding the streets, cracks. He abruptly decides to give up and leave with his men.

Several men refuse to go with him. They join Sardar. One of these men is Ali Musio; he stays behind with his two sons and his men. It was Ali Musio's courage and dauntlessness that saved Sardar's life. The enemy had completely surrounded Sardar's house when Ali Musio, who was defending the bazaars, rushed to Sardar's aid and routed the enemy from the rear.

The city is in turmoil. Bagher Khan's withdrawal allows Rahim Khan's men to enter the city without resistance. They easily capture the area of Nobaar Street and Maralaran. They had been ordered by the Russians and English not to loot, kill, or rape. It is all politics. The Russians and English want to win over the people. But the people know very well who are really their friends.

Amirkhyz, under the leadership of Sardar, alone resists. The entire country watches the small area of Amirkhyz. It holds off the shah, the Russians, and all the warlords. Miraculously, Amirkhyz does not yield.

* * *

Silence reigns over the table during dinner at the Wilsons. Appetites aren't as keen as usual. Mr. Wilson gets up and leaves the table for his favorite chair. He cleans and fills his pipe.

"It's too bad," he says, "but it will all be over in a few days."

Howard and the Wilsons accept his words, until the sounds of gunfire erupt again. Helen goes over to the window.

"It is truly a shame," she says.

"Brutality," Howard replies, "doesn't understand shame." He puts on his coat and walks out. Still at the window, Helen sees Howard cross the schoolyard, stop, light a cigarette, and vanish in the gathering darkness.

Mr. Wilson asks everyone to sit with him awhile. He has something on his mind: to talk. His gaze lingers on his wife and daughters. Speaking softly, he urges them to leave Tabriz and go back to America until things settle down. Helen rejects the idea immediately. She has no intention of leaving Howard in Tabriz. She will leave only with Howard, should he decide to leave.

Annie is also against leaving Tabriz. She feels no danger, either for her or her family. She was born in Iran, and she had always expected to die in Iran. Events prove her right. The family would move back to America, but Mr. Wilson and Annie would return to Iran. And they would die in Iran.

* * *

As he has come to expect, very few boys attend to Howard's class: Hajji Agha, Hussein Khan, the plump Tojjar and some others.

Howard says, "I think I'd like to remind you today of one of your great men, Cyrus the Great."

He reads passages from a famous address by Cyrus: "My great army moved peacefully inside the city of Babylon. I allowed no harm to come to the people of this city and the land of Sumer and Akkad. The thought of the religious places of Babylon shook my heart. I decreed that all people were free to worship their own gods. I decreed that not a single house was to be destroyed and nobody deprived of his livelihood. I decreed that all the temples of Babylon, Ashu, Shush, Akkad, and of all lands situated on the other side of Dejleh, erected in olden times and closed, to be opened. I returned all the gods of these temples to their respective places and ordered that they be preserved there always. I also returned the gods of Sumer and Akkad, brought by Nebonid to Babylon, to their proper places. I gathered the inhabitants of these places, rebuilt their houses, and granted peace and tranquility to all. The great god was pleased with me and bestowed his blessings on me, Cyrus, and on my son Kambujieh, and on all my armies.

* * *

A knock on his door early one morning awakens Howard. Hajji Agha, Hussein Khan, and four others are standing outside. They are dressed like Sardar's men. They are all carrying rifles.

Hajji Agha says, "We are ready for class, sir."

And that is how Howard went from being their history teacher to being their military instructor.

* * *

It is night. In a basement of the Memorial School, Howard's most faithful students, Hajji Agha, Hussein Khan and some others, are gathered for their nightly session on the rudiments of rifle use and battle tactics.

Howard had been a soldier. He had had only rudimentary military training himself. But under the circumstances, it fulfilled the need. The students look up to Hussein Khan. He is thought by all of them to be the ablest and bravest soldier in the group.

The sessions are a secret from everyone. No one knows of them except Howard and his students. Not the boys' parents, not Mr. Wilson, not even Helen. Should they be discovered, it would be the end of the sessions.

A guard is posted at the entrance. Schoolbooks are on every table. Should they be surprised, they hope to be able to say that were studying. The students are allowed out only because they have told their parents that classes are being held at night for reasons of safety.

But one day they are surprised by Mr. Wilson. He walks in, sheepishly followed by the student guard. Saying nothing, he looks around the room and, wordlessly, leaves.

When Howard and the boys go out, they find Mr. Wilson with a group of parents who have come to collect their sons. They all fear that Mr. Wilson has given them away. But they are mistaken.

The boys depart with their parents.

Mr. Wilson and Howard walk home to the sound of gunfire. Moonlight filters through the trees. A soft breeze caresses on their faces.

"They are concerned about their boys. I told them that you are holding classes at night for their safety."

They walk in silence for a few minutes.

"Howard, have I told you about my grandfather? He fought in the Revolutionary War beside George Washington. You remind me of him."

Howard is grateful, flattered, and uncomfortable. He hardly knows how to respond. He says nothing.

"My heart is with you, God forgive me. You must know that, son. But school is for children to learn how to read and write, for history and science and arithmetic, and for many other things. It is not a place where they ought to be taught how to kill and how to die."

"You put it so brutally! What you say is true. Indubitably true. But I am not teaching them how to kill. Surely you see that? I'm teaching them only how to fight most successfully for their cause. And their cause is just and moral. Under the circumstances, am I doing wrong?"

"My heart is with you. A more worldly man than I would not dispute you. But are we not taught to regard the things of this world with a smiling contempt? And, Howard, you've made a good many enemies at the school already. They aren't likely to hold their tongues. They will write to the Mission, if they haven't already."

Howard is silent.

"Will you think it over?"

Mr. Wilson is a good man, truly a Christian. As he watches him walk away, Howard feels overwhelmed by affection for his decent, kind, gentle father-in-law. He resolves to give Mr. Wilson's words careful thought.

* * *

Howard is on one of his late-night rambles when he sees smoke in the distance. It is thick and rising, unmistakably a scene of tragedy. Just then, Hussein Khan races past in its direction. Howard sets off in pursuit.

The source of the smoke is Ali Musio's house. It has been set ablaze. It is all too easy to guess who is responsible. Hajji Agha is at the scene.

A woman comes running out of the burning building. It is Ali Musio's wife and she is carrying a small child, badly burnt, although Howard does not know this. She falls to the ground. People rush to help her. Others, Howard among them, set about trying to put out the fire.

Ahmad, one of Howard's students, a quiet boy, rushes into the house with a heavy blanket. Someone says that Ali Musio's daughter, a little girl, is trapped within. He stumbles back with something wrapped up in the blanket. Howard, who has retreated from the blazing building, sees that it is a little girl. She seems unharmed, but Ahmad has paid in burnt flesh for his selflessness.

At that moment, Ali Musio rides up to the scene. He leaps off his horse and, after casting a glance in his wife's direction, he gathers up his daughter, who is, indeed, unhurt.

The mortally injured Ahmad is lying on the ground, screaming. Hajji Agha sobs unrestrainedly. "They can loot us," he whispers to his friend. "They can loot us. They can burn our houses. But they will not take away our will. They won't, Ahmad. They cannot! We are the wind of God, Ahmad. Can you hear me?"

Ahmad is beyond the reach of human speech. But Hajji Agha goes on, "Ahmad, we are God's wind. We cannot lose. And we will never forget you. Never."

Ali Musio is back on his horse. He looks down at Hajji Agha and the lifeless Ahmad. "You will not be forgotten, my friend," he says. "I give you my word. You will be avenged." He rides off.

* * *

Howard goes to see Mr. Sharifzadeh. He is let in by Mr. Sharifzadeh's sleepy helper. It is dark inside. The helper withdraws, leaving Howard to grope through the darkness. Howard is wondering how he is going to find Mr. Sharifzadeh when he hears the familiar, rasping tones: "Should you not be home at this hour?'

Mr. Sharifzadeh is sitting in a corner, fingering his prayer beads. His features are illuminated faintly in the flickering lamplight.

"I had a feeling that you were on your way to me. I have told you before, and now I tell you again, my friend, you must stay out of this. I know you want to meet Sardar. If you do, you will not be able to turn back. Withdraw now. Before it is too late."

Howard attempts to explain that he can be of use to the movement.

He can help Sardar organize his men and train them. Mr. Sharifzadeh tries to persuade Howard otherwise. But he knows it is useless. His parting words are, "You must let Helen know, Howard. She must know and she must agree."

* * *

Howard and Hajji Agha have come to see Sardar. Two armed men guard the entrance.

Sardar with his son at his house in Tabriz

One goes in, and from a second-floor window, he signals for the two of them to be allowed to enter. They are shown into Sardar's presence.

He is sitting on a small cushion at the end of the room, talking with a visitor and smoking his water pipe. The room is almost full of men. Hajji Agha and Howard walk over to Sardar, who rises to greet them. They shake hands and sit; Hajji Agha sits in the middle. Howard notices that everyone in the room is sitting cross-legged. He tries but can't achieve the position. Sardar smiles at Hajji Agha. "Tell our American friend, you are our guest, and a guest is a gift from God. Please sit however you are comfortable."

Howard smiles, stretches out his legs, leans back against the wall, and says, through Hajji Agha, "I am filled with joy to finally sit with you."

They talk about America's being a free country, and how it is only under such freedom that people can live well.

Sardar says, "My friend, it is only a government chosen by the people that can serve the interests of the people. That is what we are fighting for."

Howard replies, "People without hope cannot fight for their freedom. Of course, a great leader can turn the despairing into brave fighters, and gain liberty and prosperity, as George Washington did. We had to revolt against the English for our freedom. We had to pay a very big price."

Sardar smiles reflectively. He thinks how helpful Howard can be. He is curious about George Washington.

"Your Washington must have had men who were trained and skillful. Could he have defeated the well-trained English otherwise?"

"In the beginning, his men did not know anything about fighting. They had had no training, were quite undisciplined." Howard looks around the room. "They were a ragged group of unorganized and untrained men. But they learned quickly. They learned from their defeats. They fought for a just cause: an independent and free America. Like you. They fought, and in the fighting, they became a great army. In the end, the same unorganized and untrained group of people defeated the well-trained and well-equipped English army."

Sardar seems to take heart from what Howard tells him about George Washington.

Stroking his mustache, he remarks, "But he didn't have to deal with starvation."

"Actually," says Howard, "he did."

Sardar's people are hungry and getting weak. That's exactly what the Russians want.

"Whatever the cost, we must defeat them and open the roads to get food," Howard says.

Sardar, who is smoking, stops for a moment and looks around the room as he hears Hajji Agha's translation.

"We must defeat them." Howard continues. "Sardar, I am with you. I am here to help you. I will train your officers. I have been well trained in America. I have started to train some men already and I need some rifles for my men."

"Your men?!"

Howard looks around the room, and then at Hajji Agha, and reads concern on his face. He has said too much. He cannot let it be known that he is training his students. He turns to Sardar, "Some men who want to fight for their land, as you do, Sardar. I will discuss this matter only with you."

"My American friend, we have no secrets among us."

Howard looks around the room, "It is always better to be safe than sorry. A code of silence is essential in war. And we are fighting a war."

"We need plenty of educated youths to help run our country after our victory. And you are doing just that and we are already thankful for that."

His confidence growing, Howard says, "There will be plenty of time, after they are free, to get an education. As for me, I am here to help."

Sardar is pleased but taken aback by Howard's ardor. He persists in his efforts to persuade Howard that he is a young man, that this was not his fight, and that he must continue teaching.

But Howard is unyielding. "I have made my decision, Sardar. I will fight, with your permission. I will fight for the freedom of the Iranian people."

* * *

Helen is at her parents' cottage. She has grown used to Howard's nightly absences. He tells her that his contributions to Mr. Sharifzadeh's movement are purely tactical. He has told her that he will not join the armed struggle. In one corner of her mind, Helen is not convinced of the sincerity of these declarations.

Chapter Seven
Night of Purpose

Tabriz is a beleaguered city. The fighting carries on after nightfall now. The shah has sent more Russian soldiers. The city is completely sealed off.

Few shops are open. Long lines form outside every shop. Bread, fresh vegetables, fresh meat staples for most Iranians are scarce, often unavailable. People begin to hoard food. Tempers fray. The city's morale plunges again. Siege conditions set in.

The shah hopes to break the people's will by starving them. But he underestimates the depth of their passion, just as he underestimates the inspiring example set by such men as Mr. Sharifzadeh, Sardar, Ali Musio, and, increasingly, Howard.

In old Persia, the king was regarded by his people as the wisest, most knowledgeable man in the kingdom. He had also to be the fairest and the most compassionate person. He was expected to devote himself to the well-being of his subjects.

Cyrus the Great was the incarnation of this Persian ideal. When he conquered Babylon, he brought just rule to a people who had lived immemorially under tyrants. Cyrus freed the Babylonian Jews from captivity and proclaimed the sanctity of all religions.

The man against whom Sardar and Mr. Sharifzadeh and their followers were waging their struggle fell far short of Cyrus's example. To Howard, brought up on the ideas of Washington, Jefferson, Lincoln, Tom Paine and Patrick Henry, Cyrus's life spoke powerfully. Indeed, he sometimes thought Cyrus was a very American Persian king.

* * *

Late one night, Howard finds himself near Mr. Sharifzadeh's house. He sees Mr. Sharifzadeh emerge from his house into the darkened street. He is wearing flowing robes but no shoes. The sight of Mr. Sharifzadeh barefoot affects Howard oddly. He follows Mr. Sharifzadeh through several crooked alleys and narrow streets.

Walking very fast, Mr. Sharifzadeh enters a wheat field. Howard struggles to keep pace. Mr. Sharifzadeh crosses the wheat field and sets off up a rocky slope.

When Howard comes out of the wheat field, he looks for Mr. Sharifzadeh but he is nowhere to be seen. After looking around for a while, he too scrambles up the rocky slope. Tired and scratched, he reaches the top of the slope. There is no sign of Mr. Sharifzadeh. In the moonlight, he sees a small cave.

He thinks of entering it but something makes him hesitate. Tired and bewildered, he sits down on the ground and waits for Mr. Sharifzadeh to reappear. His shirt billows in the gentle breeze. He is in a very disturbed state. He shuts his eyes tightly.

When he opens them, he sees Mr. Sharifzadeh sitting on a rock high above him. A breeze lifts his scarf and plays with it. Howard is very conscious of the soft mountain breeze and the star-filled sky above. He looks around, elated and apprehensive at the same time.

Now, Mr. Sharifzadeh is no longer on the rock. But Howard catches sight of him disappearing into the wheat field. He scrambles down the slope in pursuit. He runs blindly through the wheat field and then, equally unseeingly, through the dark, empty streets and alleys. He glimpses an image of Mr. Sharifzadeh, but only for an instant.

He arrives, out of breath, at Mr. Sharifzadeh's house. It is past midnight; after hesitating, he knocks. Mr. Sharifzadeh's sleepy helper opens the door. Howard goes up to Mr. Sharifzadeh's room, and finds him sitting in the same position as when he had last seen him. He is even wearing the same cloth on his head. For some reason, the helper smiles at Howard.

He is pondering these disturbing occurrences when Mr. Sharifzadeh says, "Stop looking for ghosts. Go back and live in peace with your beautiful wife. Don't break her heart."

* * *

Mr. Sharifzadeh's helper wakes up at dawn. Sleepily, he washes his face and hands in preparation for his early-morning prayers. Muslims pray five times a day: before sunrise, at noon, before sunset, before dinner, and just before midnight.

These prayers have the effect of arresting a man's daily routine; they detach him from the material world and force his thoughts towards God. He gives his thanks to God and in these moments of stillness finds peace within himself.

The helper looks up at Mr. Sharifzadeh's window. The windows are still shut. He sees Howard's silhouette in the candlelight, pacing back and forth.

* * *

A cold breeze brushes Howard's face. He finds himself somewhere in the mountains. He looks back: nothing but impenetrable fog. Sounds of chanting fill the air. The horse under him (he becomes aware that he is riding one) is insensitive to his commands. They are traveling up a mountain road, through a narrow pass.

The sounds of chanting and music grow louder. Howard feels himself nearing their source. He doesn't know where he is or where the horse is leading him. He shuts his eyes. When he opens them, moments later, he sees a russet-colored light on the mountains. He dismounts. The horse promptly trots off. He follows. He reaches some sort of clearing. A group of people are sitting around a large fire. Its flames shoot up very high in the air, farther even than Howard can see. The people sit as if in a trance. Some are chanting; others appear to be meditating.

They are all dressed in green. An old man with a long beard plays an old Persian instrument, the sitar, and sings. Others sing with him. He is facing the fire; Howard notices that his eyes are closed. Fireballs scatter and shoot up. Howard sees Mr. Sharifzadeh through the flames and walks around the fire toward him. But when he reaches him, Mr. Sharifzadeh isn't there. This happens several times. Howard spots Mr. Sharifzadeh and makes his way to the spot, only to find when he gets there that Mr. Sharifzadeh has moved elsewhere.

No one seems to mind Howard's presence. He wonders if they

are even aware of it. Then he notices that everyone's eyes are closed. Several men fall down on the ground. Then they rise, one by one, and begin a slow dance, their eyes still closed. Some are still sitting motionless. A few are lifted into the air and slowly float back down, still in a sitting position.

Howard is very disturbed. He searches for Mr. Sharifzadeh. To no one in particular, perhaps only to himself, he whispers, "Who are these people?"

Mr. Sharifzadeh's voice whispers back, "Dervishes."

Howard looks around but does not see Mr. Sharifzadeh. Some more men fall down. Then he sees Mr. Sharifzadeh on the other side of the fire; he is being lifted into the air. His eyes are closed. He is in a sitting position, playing with his beads.

Howard whispers to himself again, "Are they dead?"

"Not in principle," Mr. Sharifzadeh whispers back. "They know how to separate their souls from their bodies. They are followers of Rumi, Omar Khayyam, and Hafez. Their bodies are left behind when their souls travel away. You must dance the *Sama*. Try."

Doubtfully, Howard joins the chanting. He tries to follow the movements of the dancers around him. Now Mr. Sharifzadeh is on a rock, his eyes closed. A thought crosses Howard's mind: Are these lost spirits?

Mr. Sharifzadeh whispers to him again. He sounds amused, "They are. I'm one of them."

By now, Howard is no longer surprised that Mr. Sharifzadeh can read his mind. Nevertheless, he decides to test him: What does Mr. Sharifzadeh think about ghosts? Do they take over your body?

Mr. Sharifzadeh laughs and whispers, "I don't know how a spirit can take over your body when you are in it. Close your eyes.

Just close your eyes."

Howard closes his eyes, still doubtful. Then he sneaks a look at Mr. Sharifzadeh.

Back comes the whisper, "Keep your eyes fully closed. Trust yourself. Let go of your consciousness and breathe freely. Allow yourself to feel the wind take your soul. You will be all right."

He shuts his eyes tightly. He allows himself to feel the heat from the flame. His face is bright red. Soon, he is weightless.

* * *

Mr. Sharifzadeh's helper sits in the yard, preparing for his sunset prayer. He looks at Mr. Sharifzadeh's window. He sees two silhouettes pacing back and forth. He rises and, smiling, goes to his room. A flock of pigeons flies over the house, heading for the mountains. It begins to grow dark as they disappear in the direction of the mountains.

Howard leans against a wall. He is exhausted. The helper hands him a glass of water. Howard drains it. Books and papers are scattered all over the room. Mr. Sharifzadeh sits in one corner, his head covered, meditating.

"It was such a long night," Howard says. Then he rises and goes out into the yard.

* * *

Howard wanders through the streets. He sees an ill-looking woman across the way. Then, he hears himself being addressed:

"Let me repair your shoe."

The speaker is an old man, almost completely toothless, by the look of it. He motions Howard to sit down, laughing all the while. Old tools and old shoes are strewn around him. Behind him there is what appears to be a potter's shop; a few old pots are visible on some shelves.

The old man chuckles, "You have a long way to go. Your shoes have to be mended."

Howard looks down at his feet. One of his shoes is split down one side. He takes it off and hands it to the humorous old cobbler.

The man says, "Take some water to that lady. She is waiting for you."

Howard picks up an old pot beside him. It is filled with water. He walks over to the ill looking woman. Propping her up, he pours water down her throat. She comes to – she had been lying unconscious and calls out his name. She reaches out to him, imploringly.

Howard looks around. The old man and the potter's shop have disappeared. He turns to the woman, who had somehow grown younger as she revived.

"What happened to the old man and the shop?" he asks.

He gets no answer. The woman has disappeared as well. He walks down the street, a nameless dread welling up inside him.

All the shops are closed. They bear signs saying "CLOSED" or "NO FOOD." Armed men patrol the rooftops. A long line has formed in front of a baker's shop. The baker comes out of his shop and shouts, "Why can you not understand? THERE IS NO BREAD LEFT! GO HOME!"

As Howard walks along, half seeing and half hearing, he is

accosted by Beerang, one of his students. It is clear to Beerang that Howard is in a bad way. He steers him gently into his family's carriage and takes him to the school.

Helen is waiting with her father and the Reverend Vanneman. They take the unconscious Howard indoors.

The Reverend Vanneman shakes his head. "I don't know if I can help him. You should take him away from here."

Howard comes to momentarily. He mumbles incoherently and lapses back into unconsciousness.

The Reverend Vanneman continues, "I have come to believe that there are lost souls wandering about here. And they can possess you."

Helen decides that she should call on Mr. Sharifzadeh. He alone, she thinks, might be able to shed light on Howard's condition.

* * *

Howard recovers quickly. A few days later, he tells Helen that Mr. Sharifzadeh has invited them to dinner.

Helen chooses her clothes carefully. She is anxious not to give offense to a man of Mr. Sharifzadeh's sensibility. She leaves no part of her body uncovered. A scarf covers her head.

Their carriage, displaying the school's flag, jolts through the streets. Recognizing the carriage, armed men along the way raise their rifles in greeting.

Mr. Sharifzadeh is waiting outside his house; the oil lamp he is carrying throws a patch of light before him. Helen knows that all the important men of the movement are targets for assassination.

And yet here he was, one of the most important figures of all, exposing himself to danger. She understands the significance of Mr. Sharifzadeh's gesture. And she is moved by it.

After exchanging greetings, they enter Mr. Sharifzadeh's house. Mr. Sharifzadeh leads them into his room, and asks to be excused briefly.

Helen takes note of her austere surroundings: books, a lantern, a few prayer rugs; that was all. Mr. Sharifzadeh returns, bearing a tray. There are three cups of tea on the tray and a bowl containing three dates. Helen is very nervous.

Noticing this, Mr. Sharifzadeh says, "I am sorry I cannot offer you more, Mrs. Baskerville. It would give me great pleasure if you were to take my share of the dates."

In the starving city, this is an act of self-sacrifice, and Helen knows it. She says, "Thank you very much, Mr. Sharifzadeh. But just tea for me, I think."

Her tact and graciousness please Mr. Sharifzadeh. "As you please, Mrs. Baskerville. Please make yourself comfortable. And let us drink our tea first. We can talk afterwards."

Helen had come expecting to persuade Mr. Sharifzadeh to release Howard. As they talk, she realizes that Mr. Sharifzadeh also does not want Howard to become involved in the struggle in Tabriz. Now Helen feels she owes Mr. Sharifzadeh an apology for having misjudged him. And casting aside the apprehension with which she had entered the conversation, she begins to confide in Mr. Sharifzadeh. She tells him about her sympathy for his struggle, the love she feels for Howard, her anxieties about him.

Mr. Sharifzadeh toys with his beads. "Mrs. Baskerville," he says, "I am not God. I am a man like Howard. I have made many mistakes in my life. My advice to the two of you, if I may give you some, is to leave Tabriz and go home. Be kind to each other. Love each other, and God will show you His kindness and His love. I shall always pray for you."

Howard knows that Mr. Sharifzadeh is right.

"You can return later," Mr. Sharifzadeh says, "when all this is over. Tabriz will still be here."

They talk into the night. When Howard and Helen take their leave, it is very late. All the way home, they say nothing to each other.

It is a night that Helen will remember for the rest of her life.

Chapter Eight
Diplomacy of Discord

As more and more men join the forces of resistance, the shah grows desperate. Acting on the advice of the Russian consul in Tabriz, he replaces the governor of Tabriz. He appoints his nephew, Einoddoleh, to the post.

He also replaces the head of the troops in Tabriz with a man named Arshadool Doleh. This man, initially a great enthusiast for the democratic movement in Tabriz, has, after marriage to the shah's aunt, changed his loyalties. He sets off for Tabriz, full of optimism that he will crush Sardar's forces.

Then the shah goes to work on the clergy. He urges them to use their influence to create disunity among Sardar's followers. Chief among these clergymen is the treacherous Muhammad Hassan Mojtahed. He and his men organize a team of assassins. Their task is to penetrate the movement and assassinate its leaders. One of these assassins is named Ahangar. He is an uneducated man, a street thug.

It has dawned on the Russian consul that force alone will not subdue Sardar and his men. Diplomacy is needed. He has had to conclude that Sardar is a much shrewder antagonist than he had originally supposed. He requests a meeting with Sardar. The request is granted, and a day is chosen for the meeting.

News of the meeting circulates throughout the city, and raises people's hopes.

* * *

Arriving at Sardar's on the appointed day, the consul is taken up to his room.

In the group around Sardar are Ali Musio and Howard. Mindful of tradition, Sardar rises to greet his guest. Everyone follows suit except Ali Musio who sits and stares resentfully.

The Russian is more than a little surprised by Howard's presence.

A water pipe is brought for the consul but he declines to smoke it.

"I'm afraid we have nothing else to offer you," says Sardar.

The Russian consul smiles. "But you do. It is all in your hands. If you put down your guns, your followers will too, and peaceful negotiations will resolve the problem."

He sips his tea and continues. He tells Sardar that people are dying for no reason, that too much blood has been shed already, that Sardar must stop.

Sardar agrees. "What you say is not unknown to us. We do not want to see our brothers and sisters killed."

"Then why don't you order your men to put down their guns and stop the massacre?"

Sardar looks around the room, first at Ali Musio and then at Howard. "We are defending our women so they are not raped and killed." he tells the consul. "So our belongings will not be torched and looted, so our people will not be killed by men sent from Tehran and by hired warlords. We are fighting to get water and food to feed our children."

Leaning forward, he continues, "You see, we are only defending ourselves against thieves, murderers and invaders. Besides, you have the ear of the shah. Why don't you have him stop?"

"Mistakes have been made, it is true. Everyone must stop together, then no one will be killed, no house will be touched. I see you are wise and brave men. If your men lay down their guns, the rest will follow."

Sardar strokes his mustache and considers the consul's words. "We will not lay down our guns," he says, "until we are sure no Russian soldier will have a foot in our land. Already, they have burned over 950 of our people's houses, including the customs at the border. They loot and kill even the animals. No one will lay down his guns until the Parliament is reopened and complete democracy and order are restored."

The consul's irritation is mounting. He is not used to such rough company or such rough quarters. Desperately, he tries to bribe Sardar: a lofty position in the army, a great deal of money.

The offer is received with sarcasm. "Thank you. But this is where you and the shah are mistaken. We are not interested in titles and wealth. We risk our lives and are prepared to die for a free and independent Iran. We will lay down our arms when the land is free of corrupt government and foreign invaders."

The consul tries to suppress his impatience. "You are making a mistake," he says. "I assure you that if you stopped fighting now, I will have a Russian flag hung from your house. No harm will come to you or your men. You will all be under the protection of the Russian flag."

But Sardar is not moved. "I know very well," he says, "how much you and the shah want me dead. But my death will only increase your difficulties. A thousand men, and more, will rise up to take my place. No Russian flag will fly on our land or from any house on it."

The consul knows that further attempts to persuade the man before him will come to nothing. He prepares to leave.

Sardar says, "You came here as a guest and our customs do not permit rudeness to guests. I cannot let you leave empty-handed. I will release some of the prisoners-of-war to you."

After directing a long look at Howard, the consul leaves.

* * *

Howard sits up abruptly in bed; Helen is asleep beside him. Howard is not wearing clothes.

This is what has awakened him: The blind, chubby-faced boy is standing in his bedroom doorway. He is wearing a long green robe; his face is shining.

Howard turns and covers Helen with the blanket and then, embarrassed and surprised, turns to the smiling boy. "Please go back to the living room! I will be with you in a moment. Please."

But the boy, who is wearing a look of great calm and serenity, says, "There is nothing to be worried about. She cannot see me. You have been a great friend. I am leaving on a long trip. I came to say goodbye."

Howard is acutely aware that he is not wearing any clothes. He pleads with the boy to wait for him in the adjoining room until he dresses. The boy regards Howard tenderly.

He says, "Goodbye, my friend. We will see each other again, I'm sure. But for now, it is time for me to go. They are waiting for me and I cannot be late. Goodbye, my good friend." Howard watches the boy walk away.

When Howard awakens, he finds no blind boy. He is being held tightly by Helen. She looks worried. He reassures her that he has only been dreaming.

He is certain that the blind boy and Mr. Sharifzadeh are somehow related. But he cannot explain this to himself, let alone to Helen.

"I am going out for a while, my love," he tells Helen, as he gets into his clothes.

Howard's nightly excursions are such a fixture in their daily lives that Helen raises no objections. But she is very worried about him. She senses that Howard is slipping away from her. She has been aware for some time that Howard's state of mind, and his feelings, are growing obscure to her. But she is helpless before the fact. All she wants is that he not slip away entirely.

* * *

The previous night's dream, or vision, is very much on Howard's mind the next day when he is wandering the streets as usual.

At Sheikh Nosrat's tea house he is surprised to see the owner sitting outside with his water pipe. He does not look happy. Two veiled women walk past the tea house.

He does not have to be at the school for several hours yet. He decides to look in on Mr. Sharifzadeh.

The situation in Tabriz has eased a little. A few stores have reopened. People are feeling hopeful. Sardar and his men have fought the enemy to a standstill.

But the city is still under siege. And the shah is sending reinforcements. More and more citizens of Tabriz are joining Sardar and his men. The main battle is still to be fought. The news of Sardar's victories has gone around the world. The newspapers that are sympathetic to the movement praise Sardar and his men. Even *The London Times*, which had always written unsympathetically of the constitutional revolution in Iran, particularly in Tabriz, has come around.

All this gives the movement much more credibility. Now, the shah and the Russians are under pressure.

The House of Constitution in Tabriz

Howard walks towards Mr. Sharifzadeh's house pondering these matters. He is distracted by sounds of a commotion. A large group is hurrying in one direction. Howard follows them. The source of the commotion is a large public assembly. People are cheering someone.

Howard sees Mr. Sharifzadeh finishing an impassioned speech to a hungry, tired and impatient audience. Moore is taking photographs on the far side of the crowd. Supporters take the smiling Mr. Sharifzadeh away.

Howard spots the thug Ahangar in the crowd. Some of his men start a fight; a few others fire their rifles into the air as they make their way towards Mr. Sharifzadeh.

Howard reaches Mr. Sharifzadeh before they do. Before he can say anything, Mr. Sharifzadeh turns to him.

"What makes you so impatient my friend? You must stop having those dreams so often."

Howard is still wondering at these words when Mr. Sharifzadeh continues, "Whatever is meant to happen will happen. So you must not try to control the inevitable. You must let nature take its course. If you try to change the course of nature the result may be less desirable for you."

Howard pulls him away respectfully. "I deserve to know the truth."

Mr. Sharifzadeh looks first at him, and then at Ahangar and his men. He turns to Howard and says: "The truth is I am leaving on a long trip. That is what you saw."

He walks away quickly and Howard follows him. "Where are you going? Why?"

Mr. Sharifzadeh says, "I'm afraid this time you have to find the answer on your own."

Mr. Sharifzadeh glances at Ahangar and his men, who are not far now. He turns his back to Howard. "Goodbye, my friend. We will see each other again, I'm sure. You have been a great friend. Would you please leave now? I cannot be late." Mr. Sharifzadeh walks away, smiling.

Howard stands still. He notices that Ahangar and two of his men are now standing before Mr. Sharifzadeh. Mr. Sharifzadeh has a welcoming smile on his face.

Too late, Howard realizes what is about to take place.

Mr. Sharifzadeh faces Ahangar.

"I am ready," he says.

Howard sees the gun in Ahangar's hand. He sees it being pointed at Mr. Sharifzadeh's stomach. He hears it go off. Then he sees and hears nothing. He stands there as the life begins to surge out of his friend.

Ahangar is surrounded. Blows rain down on him. Howard is part of this group. But instead of beating Ahangar, he takes his gun away from him.

"No," Mr. Sharifzadeh says faintly. "Do not harm him. I forgive him. Let him go free."

Howard hesitates.

"He will suffer more if you let him live. Let him go." These are Mr. Sharifzadeh's last words.

Howard returns to himself. He begins to flail his arms among the crowd. He tries to stop the beating of Ahangar. "Didn't you hear him? Let him go! Let him go!"

Ali Musio rides up to the scene. He dismounts. His face is distorted by rage and grief.

* * *

At Mr. Sharifzadeh's funeral, Howard is among a large mass of mourners. All Mr. Sharifzadeh's friends have gathered to bid him farewell: Sardar, Bagher Khan, Ali Musio, Mr. Wilson and a group of teachers from the school, and Hajji Agha, Hussein Khan and many other students.

It is a large crowd. The mood is somber. But there is rage

under the collective grief.

Howard notices a woman walking alone on the edge of the crowd. She is tall, and veiled.

Some words of Mr. Sharifzadeh come back to Howard:

"Muhammad knew he was going to be poisoned by his most trusted follower. But he let it happen. Moses knew his people would turn on him after he guided them to freedom. But he still led them to freedom. Jesus was not surprised by the crucifixion. Jesus allowed himself to be crucified for you and me. All these holy teachers could have walked away from their mission at any time. But they did not. They wanted men to have eternal salvation. All they asked us to realize is that we are the creators of our own realities.

"We do not need an arbitrator between God and mankind. You can go straight to God and talk to Him. But have we ever listened? No. Instead, we follow the monsters who guide us to kill the holiest teachers. Why? Because to accept them means to accept the truth, and to accept the truth means sometimes to deny ourselves. And to deny ourselves will lead us to deny God. Therefore, we deny them blindly. People, God just put you to the test; this is our salvation, because to accept this truth is to get to self-realization and therefore to get to God. And if we don't, we are surrendering to the fear and dependence on evil rather than love and acceptance of your own power. My friends, now, you are free to choose . . ."

When the ceremony ends, Howard looks for the veiled woman. He sees her standing alone under a tree. He forces his way through the crowd towards her. But when he reaches the spot, she is no longer there.

The revolutionaries taking the dead leader to his grave

* * *

The National Council decides to set aside Mr. Sharifzadeh's dying wish. They decide that Mr. Sharifzadeh's murderer cannot go unpunished. They sentence Ahangar to death by hanging.

* * *

Howard spends most of his days alone in the school library.

Mr. Sharifzadeh and Howard were like the philosophers Rumi and Shamas. Rumi and Shamas had, as it were, completed each other. One of them could not live without the other.

Change had come to their favorite tea house. Sheikh Nosrat

had hired a young man to perform the tasks that he had once carried out himself. Now, Sheikh Nosrat sits apart, nursing his water pipe and never saying a word to anyone.

Howard visits Mr. Sharifzadeh's grave regularly. He sees Sheikh Nosrat there once.

And one day, Sheikh Nosrat, without a word to anyone, vanishs. He was never seen or heard from again. It was if he had never been.

* * *

At the graveyard one day, Howard is surprised by the sight of a tall, veiled woman sitting beside Mr. Sharifzadeh's grave. He immediately recognizes her as the solitary woman at the funeral. Then, his memory working, he realizes that it is the same woman who handed him the bowl at Mr. Sharifzadeh's house late one night, with the single word, "ash."

He hurries towards her.

As soon as she sees Howard, the woman gets to her feet and prepares to leave. But Howard, casting aside politeness, prevents her.

"Please. Please. Who are you?" he says. "I must know. I beg you to tell me."

Meeting only silence, he tries again, "Are you his mother?"

Silence.

"He was my best friend," Howard says desperately. "I am sure you understand why I ask. Won't you please tell me?"

From behind the veil come words, softly spoken "I was his childhood playmate."

"May I see your face?"

She looks around anxiously before lifting her veil for an instant. That momentary glimpse shows Howard a face of great, sad, doe-eyed beauty. Her cheeks are wet with tears.

Before Howard can say another word, she turns and walks away quickly. He makes no move towards her, does not call after her. He would never see her again.

* * *

Mr. Sharifzadeh's death deepens Helen's isolation from Howard. Howard is almost never at home. He is restless, sleeps little, and has no appetite. She wants to comfort him but now, more than ever, is powerless to do so.

Howard's situation is like that of Rumi's after the disappearance of his friend Shamas. Rumi searched far and wide for his friend but did not find him. Without Shamas, Rumi lost the will to live.

Something like that is taking place within Howard.

* * *

Howard is thinking of the place in the mountains where he had seen people dancing and chanting around a large fire, their eyes closed. The dervishes: the word comes back to him. The place had the power to soothe and heal the spirit, and Howard had experienced it.

Now he longs to return to that spot. But he does not know the way. Mr. Sharifzadeh had always been his guide.

But one day he does find the place. By accident; he thinks: he had just been wandering in the area. In his disturbed state, Howard does not even wonder for a moment that it should have been so easy.

He sits down on the ground and shuts his eyes.

When he opens them, he finds Mr. Sharifzadeh sitting beside him. He is in a long, loose shirt.

Howard looks at him tenderly. "You knew. You knew they were going to shoot you. And you could have prevented it. But you didn't. Why didn't you?"

Mr. Sharifzadeh's manner has not changed at all. He gets to his feet and dusts himself off. "I'm afraid you will have to discover the answer to that question yourself. I have to leave. There is some gardening that I have to see to."

* * *

On another nightly ramble, Howard finds himself walking in the wheat field near his cottage. It is raining in the mountains but not where Howard is walking. Here there is a thick fog instead.

Howard has a confused sense of being followed and, even more confusingly, the sense that the waving wheat is trying to communicate something urgent to him.

He walks on.

Suddenly, men rise out of the wheat field and surround him. He thinks they might be Russians. They wave thick, wooden sticks in the air and advance towards him. There is no escape and he is hopelessly outnumbered.

He remembers Mr. Sharifzadeh's words: "A man must see within himself first; he must conquer his fears before he can take on his enemies."

Howard sits down on the ground and closes his eyes.

The stick-wielding men are momentarily surprised by this tactic, but they advance towards him nevertheless. Howard gets to his feet, his eyes still closed. They fall upon him.

He beats off the men and dispossesses them of their sticks. He begins to flail about him with the sticks. He is fighting effectively but there are too many of them. He feels his strength going. Blood flows down his face. He falls to the ground.

Just then, the sticks are plucked from his attackers' hands. And as if an invisible enemy, or enemies, were handling them, the sticks begin to beat the helpless men. Within moments, the entire group is lying on the ground, unconscious.

From somewhere, Hussein Khan, Hajji Agha, Tojjar and other students of Howard's appear. They gather around him. They are all badly bruised and bleeding. Howard greets them warmly. He tries to say more, but faints.

* * *

It is the next morning. A cold breeze on his face makes him open his eyes. He is standing in the middle of the wheat field. He checks himself out; he is in good health.

The sun tips the roofs of the houses below him. His heart and mind feel clearer than any time in the last few weeks. As if having just reached a decision, he walks firmly towards the school and his waiting students.

Howard enters the classroom to a pregnant silence. He walks up to Hajji Agha, Hussein Khan and Tojjar, in turn. He inspects them all closely. None of them looks as if he had been in a bloody fight the previous night. Every one of them has noticed the change in their teacher since Mr. Sharifzadeh's death. He looks haggard and his clothes are shabby. He looks like a man who hasn't slept or washed or changed his clothes in several days.

So much has happened to Howard recently that even the miraculous arouses no questioning in him anymore.

He walks to the front of the room and faces his mystified audience.

"I have studied and taught history in the hope that it will bring understanding."

There is absolute silence in the classroom.

"But I can no longer do so. I have nothing to teach you in this room. Anyone who wants to learn from me knows where I can be found from now on."

With these words, he walks out of the room, carrying his school chair, across the schoolyard, through the gate, and back into the troubled city.

* * *

It is a sunny day, and a soft wind is blowing. Howard places his classroom chairs in the center of the old abandoned fort. He stands alone beside his horse. The chairs are surrounded by a wall fifty feet tall. The fort is up against a mountain. Howard looks around. It is a safe place; no one can see them.

The ark in Tabriz used as a base by the revolutionaries in 1908

The ark in Tabriz that Howard and the revolutionaries used as a training base

Howard places a training sign at the base. Occasionally, he glances at the mountain of Sahand in the background. He looks out through the wide opening between the tall walls; nothing can be seen, just open land. The city lies in the distance.

He recalls all his experiences in his new host country. Mr. Sharifzadeh always made things easy for him to understand; he got to the point and made Howard see things clearly. But now, he has to discover everything himself; he has to make his own decisions without the help of his friend. He thinks he doesn't belong to this country, but he thinks all borders are set by man. Before civilization, there were no borders saying where home was. The land was home, all of it. Freedom has no boundaries.

He remembers Mr. Sharifzadeh's words and says them aloud to give them life: "Freedom is like air; it must be within a man's reach to breathe anywhere and anytime."

Howard could not let his friend down. His soul was watching him and asking him to do as his heart wished. He could not walk away from his destiny. And now, in the eyes of many, he has abandoned his school, his Church and his past. And he is about to lose his love, Helen. Everything that he has, and in which he believes, will be gone or altered forever.

How much was love of freedom really worth? What kind of value could you put on it, to make you give up everything, even your life? Freedom for a nation that you, just a few months ago, did not know. In the beginning he had just wanted to write the history of his new family. Now, he wanted to also help make it. They were his friends, and he could not leave them.

The tall walls, dark mountain and dead silence create a feeling in Howard's heart of being in suspension. As a soft breeze touches Howard's face, he notices an older shepherd walk around his horse, smiling at him. Howard looks around but sees no sheep. The shepherd walks away, reciting a poem with the confidence of one who has the answers to all Howard's troubling questions. As if in a dream, Howard follows out of the ark, without question, hearing the shepherd's words with translucent clarity.

I am a prisoner,

I am a prisoner of time,

Keep running, never stop

I am a prisoner of my mind,

Always challenge the way out

I am a prisoner of love,

Searching for the truth within one,

I am a prisoner of hope

Wishing the light will shine

I am a prisoner of doubt,

If there is right over wrong

I am a prisoner of fate,

Why must I keep belief in one?

Suddenly there is no more shepherd. He has vanished, as if he were never there. Howard finds himself some way from the ark. His horse turns and its face touches Howard's hand, as if the horse knows that Howard needs help. Howard mounts up and rides back to the ark. Dust rises about him, as he rides around the ark searching for the shepherd. Howard wonders about the shepherd or even if there was one.

Covered with dust, Howard finds himself by his chair in the middle of the ark. There is silence except for the stirring of a light breeze. He stares at the mountain. He knows his students will show up, and he waits patiently.

He closes his eyes and reflects. He has to do the honorable thing. He opens his eyes and looks up to the sky for answers, "God, I sometimes don't understand how you operate. You give power and wealth to those who are ruthless and brutal, but you don't even hear the ones who deserve your help! Can you hear me? I want to know the truth. What are these dreams? Who is controlling my fate? Is it you, God, or the devil? Can you hear me? Talk to me!" Just as he is about to close his eyes, they fill with tears, and he finds himself suddenly being yanked through a tunnel of multicolored lights.

Howard panics and screams as he zips through the tunnel at the speed of light. "Okay, I'm sorry! I'm sorry! Please let me go! I did not mean it! Please, please!"

He is suddenly dropped down onto his chair as the lights disappear into the tunnel and then into the sky. He jumps up from his chair. For a few minutes, he walks about, confused and disoriented.

He is dimly aware of shadows falling into line: Hussein Khan and some others, holding their rifles. Hussein Khan raises his rifle and signals to his friends to line up.

The boys wait for a long time. A few eagles begin to circle above the fort.

Howard rubs his eyes and begins to return to himself. He mounts his horse. He fumbles with his gun; he looks up at the mountain and then, cautiously, at the troops. He rides around, kicking up dust. He's still not completely conscious of his surroundings.

The boys stand silently and still. Hussein Khan finally says, "We are ready for training, sir."

Howard stares at them and then says, "You don't have to be here if you don't want to be. I don't want you to do this for me. I want you to be here because of you. Any of you can walk away before it is too late. There will be no embarrassment if you do. But if you want to walk, walk now."

Hussein Khan steps out and says, "It's inside our borders!"

Howard cuts in and yells, "Freedom knows no borders or boundaries! Borders are set by men. Man is born free and equal, and we will die free and equal. We will call ourselves, the Rescue

Team! This place will be our secret training place, and no one will say a word about it."

Baskerville's platoon: From left to right, standing: Motamedol Tojar, Karim Eskandani, Rezazadeh Shafagh (Hajji Agha), Hassan Kooze-Kanani, Abbasali Hariri, Reza Paknia, Zeinal Balazadeh. Seated: Karim Rafi, Ali Birang Hariri, Mohamad Ali Paknia, Ahmad Ghazvini, Ahmad Balazadej, Ali Postkaneh, Abrahim Ghafghaichi.

Howard picks Hussein Khan to be the leader of the team. They began their training. The rich boys of Tabriz not only begin a new chapter in Persian history, they are making history.

A few days later, this correspondence takes place between Howard and his father-in-law.

Tabriz, Persia, March 30, 1909

Dear Mr. Wilson,

Please accept my resignation from my position at the Memorial School. As you must have noticed, I can no longer teach history. I apologize for any inconvenience this may cause you. I am greatly needed elsewhere.

With all due respect,
Howard C. Baskerville

Tabriz, Persia, March 30, 1909

Dear Mr. Baskerville,

In reply to your letter of resignation from your position of teacher, allow me to say that I regard your contemplated course of action as unwise, rash, and impractical, as founded on a grave error of judgment and certain to lead to serious consequences to yourself and others. I, as a friend, must advise you strongly against any such course. If you acknowledge my authority, I would enjoin you from it for the common good. I regard your first obligation as to the school and still look to you to fulfill your contract as a teacher.

Yours sincerely,
S. G. Wilson

Tabriz, Persia, April 1, 1909

Dear Mr. Wilson,

Please forgive me for not taking your advice. You have my resignation.

Sincerely yours,
Howard C. Baskerville

Howard also sends the American consul the following letter:

Tabriz, Persia, April 1, 1909

Mr. W. F. Doty, United States Consulate

Dear Mr. Doty,

By order of the de facto government of Tabriz, I have taken charge of the organization and drills of the men who are defending the city. In doing this, I maintain that I am not engaging in revolution but merely acting in defense of American lives and property, as well as the lives and property of innocent Persian friends. I am not resisting any lawful government but merely helping the de facto government to defend innocent citizens from lawless looting, rape, and murder.

The situation is as follows: Tabriz is surrounded by a horde of Kurds and brigands, whose commanders are looting. One of those commanders, Rahim Khan, is openly disobedient to the shah and, avowedly, beyond his control. This is shown by the fact that last summer they looted bazaars and houses without distinction, including property belonging to Russians.

Also, lately, when they entered the west side of the city, they pillaged indiscriminately, including devoted Royalists. Rahim Khan has been systematically robbing the Russians and those who are known to be supporters of the shah. These Kurds and brigands are trying to enter the city with the avowed purpose of plundering, raping, and murdering. What reason have we Americans and Europeans to suppose that we will escape lawless raping and murder? In order that no others may be involved in this, I have taken this step without consulting with any Americans, and also, I have completely severed all official relations with the Memorial School.

Very sincerely yours,
H. C. Baskerville

Tabriz, Persia, April 2, 1909

My Dear Mr. Baskerville,

I am holding your resignation under consideration and will reply in regard to it later. Meanwhile, I should be glad to see you and talk over matters again. Come today if you can.

With salaam and prayers, yours,
S. G. Wilson

Tabriz, Persia, April 2, 1909

My Dear Dr. Wilson,

It seems to me that talking the matter over any more can only cause pain. I must do this. I should be exceedingly glad to stay out of it but cannot. Mr. Moore and I are in it for better or for worse. May God take care of us all. I feel overwhelmed by a tremendous burden which I cannot shake off, and talking would only distress me.

With many prayers and salaam.

Affectionately yours,
Howard C. Baskerville

Tabriz, Persia, April 2, 1909

My Dear Mr. Baskerville,

In accordance with your request, I regretfully accept your resignation from the position of teacher at the Memorial School, assuring you of our appreciation for your energy and devotion to your work in the past. I trust that God will bless and keep you from temptation and from dangers seen and unseen on this mission (Numbers 6:24–26), which are many. We appreciate your motives and self-sacrifice but feel that you have erred.

I remain yours sincerely,
S.G. Wilson, Principal

Howard sent his mother this letter:

Tabriz, Persia, April 11, 1909

My Dear Mother,

Before this, you have heard, probably, that I am engaged in helping those who are defending the city. The city is surrounded by a lot of barbarians whom even their leaders cannot control, and one of these leaders is openly disobedient to the shah himself. These barbarians are trying to starve the city into submission and then plunder it, not for the shah's sake but to enrich themselves with loot. Inside the city, the defenders have been doing bravely, but they were utterly lacking in organization and military training. The faculty of organization seems to be utterly absent with these Persians. Also, the defense required more leaders, men who could plan as well as command in fighting. The Persians were very anxious to get a European or American to help them, and they offered me complete charge of the organization and drilling of the forces that are defending the city. After careful thought and hesitating a long time, I finally consented, resigned from my position in the school, and now have my headquarters with the chief military leader, Sattar Khan.

At the same time, without my knowledge, an English man, Mr. Moore, a correspondent for a London paper, decided to help these fellows; so now, we are working together in everything, to bring it to a speedy close. We are drilling troops and making plans, and we hope that inside of a week or two, the siege will be raised. Possibly we may have peace in a few days without fighting. However, if these barbarians will not leave by order of the shah, we are ready to fight them, and they may be sure that they will get the worst of it.

Please do not worry about me; I am all right. Hoping to see you all now very soon, I remain, as always,

Your affectionate son and brother,
Howard C. Baskerville.

* * *

At his training ground in an old abandoned fort, Howard's thoughts turn to the past.

He recalls all his experiences in his new country. Mr. Sharifzadeh always made things easy for him to understand; he made Howard see things clearly. But now, he had to discover everything himself; he had to make his own decisions without the help of his friend. He thinks he doesn't belong to this country, but he thinks all borders are set by man. Freedom has no boundaries.

He remembers Mr. Sharifzadeh's words and says them aloud, "Freedom is like air; it must be within a man's reach to breathe anywhere and anytime."

Then he gets up from his chair and walks to his students who are waiting impatiently for him, rifles at the ready.

Chapter Nine

Absolute Commitment

From then on, Howard is completely committed to the revolution. He seldom returns to his house or to the Memorial School. Most of his time is spent training with his men or riding around with Ali Musio and his men.

Bagher Khan has rejoined Sardar and the struggle. And this raises everyone's hopes.

Helen tries to join Howard's group but Howard sends her away. One day, Helen returns to Howard's camp carrying a rifle. She thinks if she cannot change Howard's mind at least she can fight besides him. Or maybe she is hoping to change Howard's mind. But her plan does not work.

The group is distracted when Sardar and Bagher Khan decide to pay Howard and his group a surprise visit themselves.

Howard and his students await Sardar and Bagher anxiously. Helen's presence has put everyone on edge.

The two men ride up.

Bagher Khan is impressed by what he sees of Howard's students.

He had expected something shoddy and amateurish. He was not prepared for the smartly drilled group that stood in front of him.

Sardar looks preoccupied. He is still convinced that Howard would be more useful to the cause as a schoolteacher. Doty, the American consul, has been plaguing Sardar with complaints about Howard's activities. Then there are the boys' parents to consider.

They all exchange warm greetings. After the initial pleasantries, Sardar comes to the point. He tells Howard that he should perhaps reconsider his decision to participate in the struggle.

"No one," Howard says, "no one has forced me to do this. I keep coming up against people trying to convince me otherwise. I will fight by your side because I believe in liberty and justice. This land cries for freedom, and those cries penetrate my soul. I have made a hard decision, and I have spent many nights contemplating what path I should follow. I will not change my mind. Nothing you or anyone else may say will persuade me otherwise. I am holding my class here and will continue to do so; these boys are here of their own free will."

The words impress Sardar but he feels obliged to try again. "My good American friend, you are passionate. We are concerned for your life and for your family. You have a wife to be concerned about. She comes first, not our struggle. We will take care of our problems somehow. Please, think again."

But Howard is unyielding: "As for the consul, I know he has been complaining. I will talk to him. I will let him know I have made my decision. I want to fight alongside you. That is what I want most of all. And it is what my family wants. "

There is silence. Everyone's attention turns to Helen.

Helen does not want Howard to risk his life. She wants him to return to his life as a schoolteacher. She still dreams of living on a farm with Howard and bringing up a large family. But she cannot say that now, at this moment, in this gathering. A word from her and she knows Sardar would forbid Howard to join the movement as a soldier.

Howard and Helen look at each other. Tears spring to Helen's eyes. She turns towards Sardar, wanting to say the words that would not come. But somehow words comes out her. "He is fighting for all of us, sir." She is sad, more than sad, but also relieved and glad. It is what Howard wants, and she will not block his way.

Sardar and Bagher exchange looks.

"All right," Sardar tells Howard. "But you must move your training to our base as soon as possible. We will meet again soon."

Then Sardar and Bagher Khan ride away.

Howard and his men celebrate. Helen watches, tearfully.

Few days later Ali Musio rides to Howard's camp, carrying several rifles for him. He is surprised to see that Howard's team is increasing in numbers. Ali Musio cheers up the group as he tells Howard, "Sardar wants you to move your team to his camp and help other teams as well."

* * *

Support is gathering for the Tabriz movement in neighboring countries like Ghafghas and Armanestan. Supplies have been finding their way from these places, through the mountains, to Tabriz.

At Sardar's house one night, the talk turns to the subject of smuggling more guns and ammunition from these places. Everyone has thoughts on the subject. Howard offers his:

"What if we hang a foreign passenger flag on the carriage and pass it through with some passengers riding aboard?"

Sardar laughs. "It is a good idea, but where can we find foreign passengers willing to do that?"

"I can find them. I know a couple who would help me."

Every road into the city is bolted down by the shah's forces. Howard's plan is daring, but perhaps too risky. Sardar says so. But Howard persuades him in the end.

* * *

Howard is in a carriage with an American couple. They are passing through the countryside, a foreign passenger flag flying from the carriage. They are carrying contraband supplies of food and ammunition.

Thoughts of his first day in the country return to Howard as the carriage approaches the warlord's post. He sees in the distance the shah's army gathered and waiting to attack the city.

Howard realizes that the forces fighting them are even bigger than he had thought.

Howard watches, Cannons and heavily armed soldiers are everywhere in sight. He notices some Russian soldiers. The carriage is allowed to pass.

They travel through a village that is being looted. Several dead men have been hung upside down in the trees.

The carriage approaches a heavily guarded hill. Armed men

ride down to meet the carriage. They are Shojaeh Nezam's men.

Army of the shah waiting to attack outside the city of Tabriz

The shah's army during the fighting with the revolutionaries

The driver is ordered to climb down and the men set about inspecting the carriage. The driver flutters about, anxiously. He is getting on the men's nerves.

A man hits the driver in the face with his rifle. The driver falls to the ground. The man then places his rifle on the driver's chest and presses him down into the dirt. He puts his foot on the driver's bleeding face. In this pose he considers whether to shoot him or not. The driver glances at Howard and the foreign couple inside the carriage. Noticing this, the man swears at the driver. "You stupid donkey, I am not blind. No grain and no food can pass."

The shah's army closed the road to Tabriz

Locals were hung to instill fear in the people

Another man has spotted the necklace and earrings that the female passenger is wearing. He snatches at them roughly. The earrings come off. But Howard has grasped the other end of the necklace, and a struggle begins.

Yet another man, seeing this, begins to hoist his rifle onto his shoulder.

The driver shouts out, "He's an American. You will get yourself into trouble for nothing. Talk to your Khan [lord]."

He is struck in the face by a rifle once more.

The driver shouts out again to Howard. "It's not worth it. Let him have it."

Just then, a shot rings out. And Shojaeh Nezam himself, his rifle held up, is among them. He takes the necklace from his man. But Howard is still attached to the other end.

Shojaeh Nezam says, "So. We meet again. Tell me, which is more important to you? This necklace or your life?"

"At this moment," says Howard, "I do not know."

Distraction arrives in the form of a train of heavily laden mules moving slowly towards the city. The prospect of looting is irresistible. Shojaeh Nezam rushes towards the mule train to inspect and loot.

They begin to quarrel amongst themselves. Shojaeh Nezam fires into the air again. Order is abruptly restored.

The carriage driver, back on his feet, offers Shojaeh Nezam a package that he has taken out of the carriage. He looks meaningfully at Howard as he does so.

The brigand leader seems reluctant to unwrap his gift. The carriage driver takes the package back and begins to unwrap it himself, looking at Howard all the while. Howard starts walking backwards towards the carriage.

Similar-looking packages have been discovered by the brigand's men and are being opened. The opening of every package is announced by a loud explosion. Small bombs have been hidden in the packages and they go off, one after the other.

The carriage driver opens his package. The explosion kills him and Shojaeh Nezam and several of Shojaeh Nezam's men.

Amidst screams and scenes of confusion, Ali Musio and several hundred men descend on Shojaeh Nezam's forces. The air is thick with bullets. One strikes the male American, Howard's copassenger, killing him instantly.

Howard moves to the wife, who is cradling the dead man in her arms.

"I am sorry," he says, brokenly. "I am so sorry."

She looks up. "For whom? Me? Him? You? Or them?"

* * *

Doty, the American consul, is traveling through the city in his carriage. He passes the church; sounds of music and singing come from it. He passes a mosque just as people are coming out. They look hungry, exhausted, despairing.

Meanwhile, Howard is also in the area, with Sardar, Ali Musio and others.

Inevitably, their group encounters the consul's carriage. Doty motions Howard to stop. The men in Howard's group get off their horses slowly and the consul climbs out of his carriage. Greetings are exchanged politely.

It is Howard to whom Doty wants to speak. He tells Howard that he must withdraw from the movement at once. His involvement is unlawful, he is a foreigner, he has no right to meddle in the affairs of a country not his own. It is his duty as an American diplomat, Doty says, to remind Howard that he is breaking American laws. And, should Howard fall into the enemy's hands, he, Doty, would not be able to help him.

Howard has heard all this before. But he listens to Doty patiently and says, politely, that his mind is made up.

"You leave me no choice," the consul says, "but to ask that you be prosecuted for your actions under American law. You face a long stay in prison, Mr. Baskerville. Reconsider. I urge you to. Otherwise, I'm afraid I shall have to ask you to hand over your passport immediately."

He is bluffing. Howard knows that he is bluffing:

"Sir, I would rather be in a man-made jail for the rest of my life than be in jail within my own conscience, knowing I did nothing to help stop the murders taking place under our noses. You can close your eyes and do nothing, but I will not live with the faces of these dead children haunting me for the rest of my life. You are more accustomed to ignoring it than I."

Farewells are exchanged. The consul gets back into his carriage, his duty done, and drives off.

* * *

One day, Sardar makes a grand gesture. He rides into the section of the city where the Russian flags are thickest. Sardar stops and looks at the rows of white Russian flags posted atop the houses and businesses. Sardar aims his rifle and shoots the first flag down. The flag lands in a small, dirty puddle.

Ali Musio replaces it with a freedom fighter's flag. Sardar turns to an old woman who is watching and yells to her:

"Mother, now you are under my protection. Not a white bear."

The old woman dances and cheers in the street. Sardar's troops take off down the street. He and his men shoot at the flags and pull them down methodically.

This was after the Russian consul had decided to meet Sardar personally. His decision was based on desperation. He had tried everything to defeat Sardar and his men but nothing had worked. He was disappointed with the shah's army and the warlords who were now in the shah's pay. So he decided to meet Sardar himself and use his professional charm and expertise to persuade Sardar to give up. He had even offered Sardar a high post and a big salary. But he had been rebuffed by Sardar. Sardar had told him that unless they were withdrawn, the Russian soldiers would be massacred.

Howard had enjoyed watching Sardar embarrass and humiliate the Russian consul. And Howard's presence during that scene had enraged the consul even more.

And now Sardar goes further and decides to eliminate the Russian flags from the houses. It is an audacious act of defiance, of course. But it is even more than that; it is a powerful signal to those who still doubted the determination of Sardar and his men.

Their bold move attracts more people to the movement. And the Russian consul, taken by surprise, petitions the shah for reinforcements.

* * *

A couple of men ride through the rain, quietly and cautiously. When they reach an abandoned building, they get off their horses. They creep through a riverbank and then down some small alleys. They are checking on the enemy's forces and seeking some way for supplies of food to get through the enemy's lines into the city.

One of the men is Howard. The fighting has intensified since Howard joined Sardar. Hajji Agha told Helen that Sardar always wants Howard by his side.

Howard has been spending most of his time at Sardar's house. Sardar likes that because when the situation worsened, when Sardar was worried or when his spirits drooped, he likes to talk to Howard. And Howard would tell Sardar about George Washington who had routed the English and driven them out of America. He even makes up an occasional story to raise Sardar's spirits.

And Howard, in turn, is impressed by Sardar's tactical shrewdness and his bravery. He comes to admire Sardar deeply. Their admiration is mutual. Sardar and his men need Howard's formal military experience.

Wandering in the dark, Howard begins to wonder what he has gotten into. He had come to Persia to be a teacher and to meet a beautiful Persian girl. Instead, he has met Helen, fallen in love, and joined the revolution. He begins to think about Helen. He has not seen her much during the past few weeks and feels guilty. But he knows he has work to do. He imagines Helen′s sitting by the fire waiting for him as she looks out of the window.

Howard is torn away from his thoughts by Ali Musio, who grabs him and pulls him away from the middle of the alley. They walk quietly through the pouring rain.

They finally stop at a small house on the hills. A man sits on the roof looking out. The gleam of light on a white Russian flag can be seen through the pouring rain. Ali Musio climbs up the wall, takes down the white flag, and throws it away. The white flag lands on the soaked ground. On the other side they can see the shah's massive army at rest.

Ali Musio climb ups to the roof and struggles with the guard. He finally kills him and throws his body to the ground. But in the process the guard's rifle goes off, raising an alarm.

Several men run out to check. They notice Ali Musio and

Howard disappearing in the rain. They begin to follow them.

The chase leads through many creeks and across fields of thick trees. Howard follows the shadows in front of him. He is soaking wet. He hears several gunshots as he reaches an old bridge almost covered by the rising river. The bridge looks as if it might be washed away at any moment.

A man is lying motionless on the bridge. As Howard runs past the man, several boards collapse under him. He is almost in the river, but manages to grasp a loose board and hold on as he dangles over the side. When he attempts to hoist himself up, the bridge begins to give way even more. The dead man's body rolls off the bridge into the water.

Howard becomes aware that Ali Musio is trying to reach him, but the bridge is giving way. Howard is hanging on for his life. Helen appears in Howard's thoughts, and he wonders what she is doing now and whether he would see her again.

Howard is pushed farther down. The struggle is draining his strength; he is approaching exhaustion.

Ali Musio is attacked by the enemy and driven off. He thinks Howard has fallen into the river. The bridge is about to collapse. Howard's strength is failing fast. Suddenly, a hand reaches down and pulls him out of the water. He looks up and catches, or thinks he catches, a glimpse of Mr. Sharifzadeh's face. But the bridge is crumbling and he has to make his way safely to land again. He begins to reflect on his mysterious savior and wonders if Mr. Sharifzadeh is really dead.

Then he notices a man walking into the woods in the distance. The rain seems to be having no effect on him. Howard gets up and follows the man. He can see very little in the pouring rain. Howard follows the man up the hill with the last of his strength.

The man turns and looks at Howard. He pushes open the courtyard door to Memorial School. Weakly, Howard follows him. He does not realize that he is at the Memorial School.

Mr. Wilson empties his pipe into a now-full bowl of burnt tobacco. He has his boots and raincoat on, and he sits by the door. He has gone out in search of Howard several times. Ali Musio has stopped and inquired about Howard but was unforthcoming about Howard's activities that night.

Mr. Wilson is worried, but he keeps his thoughts to himself; he has told Helen nothing. Ali Musio and his men are also looking for Howard now. Sardar was worried that something had happened to Howard; his men scour the city in search of him. Helen sits by her father on the couch and stares worriedly out the window. Her father paces the room, making her even more nervous.

Howard enters the Memorial School courtyard hardly able to stand on his feet. He is dripping wet; he sneezes several times. He slowly makes his way through the courtyard; a tiny light appears in Mr. Sharifzadeh's old classroom. A shadow walks back and forth across the room. Howard calls out Mr. Sharifzadeh's name softly. He is so weak that he can barely form the words. His hands are shaking badly, and he can only just keep his eyes open. He falls to the ground and loses consciousness.

Helen sees Howard enter the courtyard and rushs out immediately. He is too heavy for her to carry. As she turns for help, she sees her father already on his way, holding a blanket. He covers Howard with it and they both carry him inside. They lay him down by the fireside. Helen calls her mother; she can tell Howard has a high fever and is breathing with difficulty.

Annie and Susan walk down the stairs half asleep, but the sight of Howard lying unconscious jolts them awake. Annie begins to spoon-feed him medicine. She covers him with blankets, and tells

Helen to lie very close beside him to warm his body. Mr. Wilson rushes out to fetch the doctor.

By now, Helen knows Howard well. She knows he always exaggerates his colds and coughs; he is a very emotional person. His theatrics used to make her laugh. But she knows that this time something is wrong. As Howard fades in and out of consciousness, he babbles to himself in a very low voice. Helen tries to make out the words but cannot. She shakes him gently but gets no response.

Mr. Wilson and the doctor arrive. Mr. Wilson adds more wood to the fire as the doctor begins to examine Howard. He gives Howard an injection. He smiles and turns to Mr. Wilson, who is sitting beside him. Howard will be all right. Before leaving, he hands Annie some medicine.

Helen keeps watch at Howard's side. Her father has gone up to bed and her mother and sister have fallen asleep beside the fireplace. Helen wipes the sweat off Howard's brow. Howard regains consciousness and begins to ramble again. Helen cannot follow what he is saying.

It is afternoon of the next day and Helen has not left Howard's side. It is raining still. Helen cries softly.

Howard opens his eyes and finds himself in a small, barely furnished room built of solid stone. A warm, large sheepskin is draped over him. He discovers that there are no signs of sickness in his body from the previous night's encounter on the bridge.

Wonderingly, he gets out of bed and walks out of the room into a thick fog outside. His arm is grasped roughly as he is about to take another step. He looks down and sees that he would have walked off the edge of a steep mountainside.

Howard turns and sees the owner of the arm that had held him back: an old blind shepherd with a white beard. He is wearing a long, loose flowing green garment. He holds a cane before him, and his feet are bare.

Howard is standing near the summit of a mountain. Below him, he sees that houses have been built into the mountainside, up to the top.

House built in the rock

Howard looks around, but sees no road, path or trail that would take people up to their houses and down the mountain.

There is a noise behind him. He turns, expecting to find men and women but sees only sheep and goats.

"Where am I?" he asks the blind shepherd.

"Nowhere."

Howard surveys the landscape before him. He turns to the blind shepherd but finds that he has disappeared. He goes back into the room to look for him but the old man is not there. He comes out and searches for a path that would take him down the mountain. But there is nothing.

Below him, people are walking about with their animals. Howard cannot see how he will find his way to them. The blind shepherd reappears, a short distance away. Howard hurries towards him.

"Who are you?"

"Like you," answers the blind shepherd, "nobody."

The soil on the mountain is reddish. All around Howard, people are applying a paste, made of the red earth and water, to their faces. The blind shepherd is doing this himself. Then a man wanders in from nowhere, talking to himself.

I am a color
Red as fire
Blue as water
Brown as earth
White as snow
Black as night
Green as a wheat field
Silver as a star
Orange as a sunset
Gray as a cloud
Yellow as a volcano
Colorless as a wind
I am as colorless as all
I am as colorless as
Man must become

The man smiles at Howard and wanders away. Howard realizes his whole body is covered with the red dye-like substance.

"What is this color?" Howard asks the shepherd.

"There is no color. Everything is colorless."

Howard looks around. "Then what is this red dye on everyone's hands and faces and on me?"

The shepherd looks into running water. Howard follows after hesitating momentarily. He is surprised to see that there is no sign of red dye on his face or the shepherd's. He touches his face; his hand is covered with red dye. He looks into the water again; there is no red dye on his face. Confused, he turns to the shepherd.

"Your eyes are deceiving you," the shepherd says. "Look with your heart and your soul."

For some reason, the thought of the Garden of Eden enters Howard's mind. He feels his skin prickle.

"What is this place?" he asks. "How can you walk from fog to rain and from the rain into the sun and from the mountain onto flat land?"

"How can you awaken from sleep and feel you are healthy and alive?" responds the shepherd.

The old man closes his eyes and applies the paste to his eyelids. Howard does the same. A cold breeze on his face makes him open his eyes. He is standing in the middle of the wheatfield. The sun touches the roofs of the houses below him. His heart and mind feel clearer than they have in the past few weeks. As if having just reached an important decision, he walks firmly towards the school and his waiting students.

* * *

It is late the next night. Helen wakes up and looks around, but Howard is nowhere to be found. Little twinges of alarm go through her. To calm herself down, she goes to the window and looks out. It has stopped raining.

She walks through the silent house. She notices a note on the table.

It is from Howard. "My love," it reads, "you are my wings. You are my angel. Without you I was lost. Your thoughts and love are what keep me going. I guess God wants me healthy to go on with my mission. Please forgive me. I had to leave. Sardar was in trouble."

But in her heart she knows Howard is long gone. She knows but can not bring herself to accept the fact, even though she knows that Howard has joined Sardar and became one of his closest advisers and most trusted friends. Hajji Agha used to bring Helen all the news he had. Howard knew that Hajji Agha did this but he never mentioned it. Hajji Agha also took messages from Helen to Howard.

But Howard and Hajji Agha were far away. They were making their way to the battle through a heavy fog.

* * *

Cigarette smoke rises from the rooftops and melts into the rain. Sardar sits exhaling smoke and looking up at the sky. He begs for help. People are dying everywhere. He does not know how much longer he can withstand the suffering around him. His mind is filled with the cries of dying babies and the imploring faces of their helpless mothers.

The rich and powerful of Tabriz are getting restive. Their frustration with the movement is mounting, and they are beginning to change their minds about it.

Without telling anyone, Sardar decides to attack Rahim Khan, the ruthless warlord. His aim is to break the siege so that supplies of food could get through to the city. But he is deceived and led into a trap, and his forces are badly defeated. Howard and Hajji Agha make their way to Sardar, who is still within view of the battlefield. He is the picture of grimy frustration, for he lost many men. He and Howard stare at each another.

Finally, Howard says, "You must leave. They will soon realize there are only a few of us left. They'll kill you. They will kill us. And that will be the end of the movement; so you must stay alive."

Enraged, Sardar points to a slain Gorjestanian man in the field. "How could I forgive myself if I left his body to the enemy? It should be returned to his country, to his mother. That is the least I can do for him. After all, he is our guest and my friend. I won't leave without him!"

His words make Hajji Agha nervous.

Sardar whispers, "Perhaps you should leave. It would be better. I will be back after dark if it is God's wish."

Howard lets him know they will not leave without him.

Rahim Khan's men enter the field and begin to methodically loot the corpses.

Sardar knows what is passing through Howard's mind. He whispers, "Then we will wait until dark."

The three wait a couple of hours. Howard tells Sardar stories of George Washington's daring. It does Sardar good to hear these stories of English defeats. The English, like the Russians, were no friends of Sardar's.

They wait late into the night. Hajji Agha's anxiety is all too evident. He expects to be killed at any moment. Howard is aware that his young friend is very tense but says nothing.

A moment later, they hear a noise. Then they see Sardar signaling for them to follow him. Howard and Hajji Agha follow Sardar, wondering where they are going. After a few minutes, they reach a spot where several horses are standing together. The

Gorjestanian's body is draped across the back of one horse.

The three get on their horses and ride away, barely able to make out the road in front of them. When they reach the bridge, they are surprised to see that a mass of people have gathered and are waiting for them. There must be several thousands of them. The crowd cheers when they see Sardar, and the sound fills the whole city. This incident would become part of Sardar's legend.

* * *

Howard has other experiences with Sardar, who reminds Howard of an American Indian named Wind. So he nick-names Sardar the wind.

Howard, Sardar and Hajji Agha ride into the village of Khateeb halting near 100 or so men who are taking cover from heavy cannonading by the enemy. A group of interested reporters join them, waiting for further developments.

Ali Musio approaches Sardar and points to a cannon on a high hill.

"The damage comes from those cannons on that hill. No one can get close." Bodies are scattered across the field. Sardar walks up to the body of an elderly man who had been a close friend. He closes the man's eyes. Cannon fire lands near him, killing more men. Sardar rises calmly and walks to his horse, staring at the hills. Howard and Ali Musio mount their horses as Sardar mounts his. He sets off with Howard; Hajji and the rest follow.

They pass through the narrow alleys separating the fields. Sardar, Howard, and Hajji are ahead of the rest. They come to an open area and Sardar rides quickly up a hill. He turns his head and sees Howard riding alongside. They ride together at full speed. Sardar tosses a rifle to Howard. Bullets and cannon fire seem to come at them from all directions, but they remain unharmed.

Ali Musio rides past Hajji Agha, who looks back fearfully but sees no one in pursuit. Sardar gallops far ahead, aims his rifle and shoots into a foxhole. Howard and Ali Musio follow, shooting. But they are far behind and they watch as Sardar reaches the top. Now, there is no cannon fire.

Hajji Agha rides nervously behind, shooting randomly into the air and dodging incoming bullets. Howard reaches the top, followed by Ali Musio and Hajji. Sardar stands calmly next to the smoking cannon and its dead crew. As Ali Musio chases the remaining enemy soldiers away, Sardar's other men arrive.

"Sardar, you must stay alive. You can't endanger yourself like that," Howard says.

"If I do not endanger myself, how can I expect my men to endanger themselves?"

Sardar walks up to the balcony of a house overlooking the river and the Russian border. A man brings Sardar a fresh hookah left behind by the enemy. Sardar smokes.

The reporters arrive and begin to take pictures of Sardar. Among them are Moore and a reporter from the *Paris Herald.* A cannon shot from the Russian side of the river rips right over Sardar's head and hits a rocky area. Debris falls. Everyone scatters for cover except Sardar, who remains seated, calmly smoking his hookah.

The reporters and others return to check on him. Dust and debris are strewn about Sardar, who serenely continues to smoke.

"Why didn't you run?" asks the Herald newspaper reporter.

"If I ran, the bullet wouldn't return to the gun, would it?" Sardar strikes a match and relights the pipe. He brushes the dust from his trousers.

Chapter Ten

Reflections on Revolution

The ways into the city remain blocked by the shah's forces. Supplies of food cannot get through. And the city continues to starve.

Howard rides through the city with a couple of his men. Civilian gunmen rest on rooftops and in street foxholes. All the stores are closed. Signs in store windows read NO FOOD. The once vibrant city has become a ghost town.

Starving people gather around the bakery hoping to get a loaf of bread. The owner comes out and shouts that there is no bread; he tells them all to go home. But no one seems to hear him. A man forces his way inside the store. He is stopped by another man and a fight breaks out. A collective rage grips all these hungry people. Some bystanders are caught up in the brawl.

Howard sees a little girl pull up some grass and eat it. Her mother hurries over and takes the grass from her mouth.

Then some other people begin pulling up grass and eating it. Howard gets down from his horse and walks over to the group eating grass. He too, takes a handful of grass and eats it. He simulates great enjoyment. He is joined by his men. Soon the brawling in the bakery comes to an end and people begin drifting over to the crowd of grass-eaters. The field is full of starving people. A few days later the field had been picked clean of grass.

* * *

Howard sits alone on a rooftop. He looks into the distance as the moon lights up the city. Each star in the sky reminds him of a lost love. He thinks of Helen, Mr. Sharifzadeh, his mother, and his sisters. Everyone he ever cared about seems to be looking down on him from above.

Howard leaves the rooftop and heads down the street. As he makes his way, he hears a weak cry from within a small, dilapidated house. A young girl comes out carrying a child. It is difficult to say who looks weaker, the child or the girl carrying her. They look faint with hunger. The girl staggers past Howard before collapsing a few steps later.

Howard reaches her as she loses consciousness. He takes the child from her and realizes that she is not breathing. He is at a loss. He begins to walk aimlessly, like a lost man.

Moments later, he finds himself standing outside the Russian consul's house. He knocks furiously and an Iranian guard opens the gate. Howard tries to get by, but the guard will not let him pass. The two men just stand there for a moment, staring at each other. Loud music is heard from inside the house; the sound pours into the streets. The guard looks at the child, and an expression of despair fills his face. He debates whether he should let Howard and the dead child pass through, but he is also worried about losing his job.

Howard looks at him and then at the girl. Nothing has to be said. The guard looks inside and then at Howard. He whispers, "You cannot get through here. Go around, I will open the back door for you."

Then he shuts the gate and whispers to himself, "Who cares if I get killed or lose my job? But God is great. He would not hurt my family for doing something good."

Soon the guard appears at the back door to let Howard in. He watches Howard carry the child into the yard and up some stairs to the house. Several dogs are being fed by workers. They take note of Howard's presence but ignore him. The guard is relieved and wonders why he had hesitated at all to let Howard enter. A party is in progress inside. People are dancing, drinking, and eating. There is an enormous amount of food, much of it going to waste. Barbecued deer, goats, and ducks lie on a long table. Howard considers God's justice.

The music comes to a stop and is replaced by a tense silence.

Howard sees the Russian consul feeding raw meat to his two fat dogs. The consul and Howard exchange a hard stare. A doctor, a guest at the party, takes the child from Howard. He places her on a table.

Howard says in a weak - stern voice, "Don't bother; she's already dead - from starvation. Why should you people care? Drink your wine and eat your food."

Then he turns to the Russian consul. "I apologize for interrupting your festivities, but I am just wondering what the consul is going to do for the people outside who are just waiting to die? Drink more to celebrate their loss? That is an excellent idea; let's all have a toast for genocide! After all, you do not live in the same world as the people of Tabriz, so why should you worry yourselves with this dead child?"

Before the Russian consul can reply, Mr. Doty cuts in, pipe in hand. "I apologize. Please let me handle this."

He steps close to Howard and says softly, "Mr. Baskerville, what are you doing here? I hope you know you are embarrassing me. We had this discussion before, several times. My hands are tied. As I said, the men are free to choose to live, and I hope they do, quickly."

Howard is furious. "These people do not choose life by giving in; they choose death. You are just a slave if you are bound by a dictator's rule, a dictator that is responsible for rapes, murders, looting, and the oppression of their women. They are sacrificing their children for the chance to be free. You see, Mr. Doty, hope is not a sufficient strategy. You cannot close your eyes. You must interfere to help these children of God and stop this madness; otherwise you are a part of it by doing nothing and by attending the party of the man who is fully responsible for this catastrophe and injustice."

Doty looks around the room, angry and embarrassed. Several Russian guards enter the room. They stop near Howard.

"I understand your concern," the American consul says. "But what you are asking me to do is against American foreign policy at this current time. I have no power to stop it. And you'd better leave before there is more embarrassment for me and you. This is a wrong place and absolutely a wrong time for such discussion, especially when you are an unwanted and an uninvited guest."

Howard shouts. He wants everyone to hear his words. "Are you people against freedom and justice? You are people, aren't you? Speak up from your hearts. Do we allow innocent people to be murdered?"

Doty speaks soothingly: "Mr. Baskerville, the Constitution of America strongly prohibits our interference in the internal affairs of other countries; therefore, there is nothing I can do. And you better leave before you are thrown out."

Howard addresses his appeal to the other guests, "Ladies and gentlemen, Thomas Paine was an English citizen and was committed to English law. But when it came to justice and human rights, he took up his rifle and joined George Washington to fight against his own country, England. Do we say that he acted unlawfully? No. When the French noblemen Lafayette and Rochambeau joined George Washington to help the Americans gain their independence, did we ask if they broke the law? No, we welcomed their help, as these people will welcome yours."

Doty cuts Howard off. "Mr. Baskerville, you might be right theoretically. But the practicality of the matter at this time is that we are not permitted to intervene. My job is to execute the law, not to make it."

Howard picks up the dead girl and turns to leave. "Your job is to help us find a way to be practical, to be human. And for sure, your job is not to attend the celebration of death and destruction of your host country."

The Russian guards surround Howard and lead him out of the house. As Howard walks past him, the Russian consul throws more meat at his two fat dogs.

He passes the guards waiting outside. Several men come out of a storage room. They are bringing more food in to the party. The sight nauseates Howard.

Howard walks down the street, still carrying the girl, and finds himself in front of a church. He enters, feeling lost and confused, needing God's help tremendously. As he makes his way down the aisle, he sees an elderly beggar ahead of him, carrying a gnarled wooden cane. The weak light from burning candles illuminates their approach to the sculpture of Christ. In the silence of the dim church, Howard hears the soft voice of the beggar, talking to his gnarled cane.

Talk to me God
How can we put love and trust
Back into men's hearts?
Men who have been driven
To hate, kill and destroy?

Talk to me God
I am lost between right and wrong
Hopefully the answers will come
Before I depart from earth into the sun

Talk to me God
I am long waiting to hear from you
and become one with spirit and light
as I depart into the colorless of internal light

Talk to me God
I am confused and lost
Talk to me God

The beggar disappears into the blackness beyond the candles′ glow, adding to Howard′s many unanswered mystic questions. Now Howard find himself standing by the sculpture of Christ. With tears in his eyes, Howard places the dead child under Christ′s statue and kneels. He begs his beloved Christ for answers. He feels estranged from mankind and longs to have all the madness around him explained. He is overwhelmed by the certainty that Christ can hear him.

"I am confused. What has happened to the judgment I was told I would find? Where is the justice I was told sinners would face? Please talk to me, my Christ. I am lost."

Tears run down Howard's face as he begs for forgiveness, freedom, and answers, as his life passes through his mind. Tears begin to well up in the eyes of the statue of Christ. They run down the statue and fall around Howard on the floor.

Suddenly, Howard feels dissociated from his body; he cannot sense his body, cannot feel it. His head begins to double over and he drops down the steps as if he were dead. He is unconscious again, and experiencing feelings that hadn't existed since Mr. Sharifzadeh's death. He is pure and calm, free of fear, sadness, and hate. An overwhelming feeling of love fills his body and seeps through his pores. He knows he will rise and shine brightly like one of the stars.

* * *

Neither the moon nor the stars are visible on this dark night. Howard finds himself at his favorite mountain slope in total darkness. A few minutes of hard climbing takes him to the top. He stands before the entrance to his favorite cave.

He walks inside, lighting matches along the way. The matches flare briefly, and then go out. He begins to lose heart in the darkness. He longs for light. He tells himself to be brave. He feels as if he were at the bottom of a deep hole. He prays for help.

An old man resembling Mr. Sharifzadeh sits in front of him. He is holding an enormous cobra. The man looks pleadingly at Howard. Howard stares, frightened, by the man and his snake.

The cobra rises and the old man walks away into the dark.

Howard senses that he will have to fight the snake. But he has no weapons. He trips and falls as he turns. He tries to run, but the old man's voice, piercing the darkness, forces him to stop. "It is too late to question your fate if you must die. Doubt only weakens you if you run."

Howard looks around, but the old man is gone.

He turns and sees the snake rising into the air to strike. He looks around and sees no way out. Sweat drips down his neck. His heart begins to race. He feels his mouth open and hears himself shout, "You can't hurt me! Go away! Go! You cannot hurt me!"

He remembers what Mr. Sharifzadeh had taught him. He must stay patient and calm; he has to focus and gather all his energy. He waves both his arms at the snake. Then he flings one arm out.

His action generates a vibrant light. It comes from deep within the core of his body and heart. It flows from his center and throughout his entire body and soul. It grows in intensity as it streams down from heaven and runs down his spine in a blinding brightness. It comes up through the soles of his feet and runs up his legs. These streams meet at his pelvic center and form a swirling vortex.

Suddenly, a concentrated beam of silver, white, and green specks shoot like a laser beam out from his pelvic center and into the serpent. The light engulfs the snake, dissolving it on the spot. The light then turns to a smoky mist, and all is calm.

When the smoke clears, Howard finds himself sitting safely atop a narrow rock. His legs are crossed, and his eyes are still closed. He is deep in meditation, illuminated by waves of green light. Soon another wave of energy rise up around Howard in time to lift him up before he can react. When he opens his eyes he finds himself floating in the air, traveling through the clouds. He is being escorted by two angels wearing blue and green silk gowns. They smile at him reassuringly. Howard feels complete peace for the first time.

He lands on the site of an ancient building in the middle of nowhere. He is surrounded by 3000-year-old temples, a castle, and a demolished building. The two angels, holding a scroll, reappear. There is a work of art upon it, like an intricate painting, but in a script that is obscure to Howard. He looks hard but cannot understand the writing, a combination of Arabic, English, and several different alphabets. It is perfectly straight in organized lines, and only in the bottom left-hand corner is there a mark that looks like the English letter "y" to break the balanced structure.

Howard examines it more closely. It looks like a Persian miniature painting. Before Islam came to Iran, paintings were mostly of men and women and sometimes contained nude figures. Those paintings were proscribed after the conquest of Iran by Islam. But Iranian painters went on painting, and the beautiful Persian miniature was born.

Howard wonders what the writing means. The angel in blue says, "This is the name of God."

If that is the name of God, thinks Howard, why don't I recognize it? Why can't I read or understand it at all? Why are they showing me the name of God?

The angel in green says, "This is the form of God."

Howard looks at the statue that the angels are pointing to: a figure, in brass, of a man covered in a brownish mold. It has fallen apart almost completely, but the right side of his face is iridescent.

Howard moves to see the other side of the face. But each time he moves, he can see only the right side. He tries to look at it from the front but cannot see the other side. He constantly sees the same shape, size, and color.

He turns to the angels in frustration. "What kind of game is this? What do you want from me? Why me? Do you know what my mother, my sister, or Helen would do if I told them you've shown me the name of God or the form of God? They'd laugh at me! They'd all think I am mad."

The angels smile at Howard. The one in blue asks, "What if we try to see what you will find out?"

Before Howard can think or talk he is up in the blue sky, traveling with the angels at the speed of sound. It is as if he is riding on a powerful wave in a stormy ocean. He is calm.

Soon, Howard finds himself at his family's farm in Nebraska. He is sitting with his mother in his old room. His sisters come in.

The angels stand in the background, watching calmly. They can read his mind and gesture to him to speak.

"Mother," he says slowly, "two angels took me to an ancient castle. I don't know where, but it was old and abandoned. They showed me the name and form of God. It was interesting. And now, they have brought me here."

His mother and sister's look at him as if he were mad.

Howard turns to the two angels. "I told you. They think I am mad."

The angel in green smiles. She says, "Shake the bedspread."

Howard looks doubtful. The angels tell him again to just shake the bedspread and watch.

His mother finally finds her voice. "Who are you talking to, Howard?"

Howard realizes they cannot see the angels. He points to the angels, "Green and blue angels! They are standing right there by the door. Perhaps you cannot see them, but you must believe me. They want me to shake the bedspread for you to see that I am right. Can't you see them?"

His words worry his mother even more.

Howard begins to shake the bedspread up and down. As they watch, fire blazes up from its center to the top. Flames of red, green, and blue illuminate the entire house. But the fire is contained in the center of the bedspread. Howard's mother faints. His sisters are frozen in shock. Howard moves the bedspread once more. The fire circles around him, covering him entirely. And he gets lost within it.

Helen jumps up and runs to the bed, shocked to see the bedspread jumping around on fire. She watches as the bedspread calms down and reassumes its original form on the bed. Steam rises from it and dances out through the window. She moves to the window and watches the steam float toward the mountain.

The steam makes its way to Howard, who is still sitting on a narrow rock overlooking the valley, meditating. He hears the elderly man's voice again. "The second chapter of the book of Genesis gives a geographical description of Eden - the Garden of Eden."

Howard looks up. He sees an elderly man sitting on the rocks above him, looking at the valley of Tabriz. He is wearing worn-out clothes and looks cold. A greenish blue light surrounds the elderly man. The light is dancing, to warm him up.

He turns to Howard. Howard hears his thoughts in his mind. Tabriz is the Garden of Eden and the old man is asking Howard to see it. Howard sees only the dark city of Tabriz.

The elderly man is persistent. "God planted a garden in the

east of Eden, with a soul which can grow every kind of tree, with every kind of fruit good to eat, with the tree of life in the middle of the garden and the tree of knowledge of good and evil. A river which flows from Eve to water the garden, is divided wide into four broad heads. The first one, named Persian, flows to the land of Hapilan, rich with gold. The gold of this country is pure. The second river is named Gihan. This one runs to the land of Kush. The third river is called Hitaped. And this flows to the east of Asho. The fourth river is the Peda . . . and there you are looking at the Garden of Eden."

But Howard still sees nothing, "If the Bible is correct, and the valley of Tabriz is supposed to be the Garden of Eden, then where is it? Why haven't I seen it yet?"

"First, man must see it within himself, not with his eyes."

Howard closes his eyes and tries to concentrate. Within a few minutes, he feels a cold breeze flowing around him. When he opens his eyes he realizes that it is no longer night.

An amazing scene lies before him. The entire valley has been transformed into a beautiful garden, a garden full of every kind of fruit tree - apricot, apple, orange, pomegranate, cherry, grape, and many others. Flowers of every kind fill the landscape. Four rivers run down the mountain, through and around the garden and then, joined together, run down to the sea.

An image from deep within the forest shows up from beneath. Howard looks more carefully and sees that the image looks like Mr. Sharifzadeh trimming a flower bush. Many other images of men and women can be seen; were they all inhabitants of this garden?

Howard begins to understand more. He whispers, "If this is the Garden of Eden, the birthplace of Adam and Eve, they must be somewhere around here. And the city of Uromyeh . . . by the salt lake, it must be here."

Then he turns to the elderly man as he continues, "That is also mentioned in the Bible."

But the old wise man is gone. Howard looks down to find that the Garden of Eden has vanished too. Below, he sees, through the darkness, only the familiar sight of the valley of Tabriz.

A strong breeze pushes him off the rock as his eyes open and he begins to fall.

Howard jumps up, awakened by the Reverend Vanneman. It is the next morning. Howard is not sure whether he ever left the church. They look at each other for a long time.

The Reverend Vanneman breaks the silence. "Is something troubling you, Howard? Maybe you need a confession. Maybe you just need a friend to talk to."

Howard gets to his feet. He feels lost and frightened. He wonders whether he is dead or alive, and whether what he is experiencing is a dream or reality. Then suddenly Howard reels out of the church as if drunk, and his strong voice surprises the Reverend Vannema.

I tried and tried, to find the truth
I sang and sang, to feel the love
I wrote and wrote, to understand the just
I looked and looked, to see the light

But every step of life, I came to a stop
I closed my eyes, to dream it all
Just to see into the mirror of life
I am old, tired, confused and lost

Suddenly a voice whispers from within the dark
Lighting within me, lands in my heart
Stop wondering, take a right step for once
Look within you, all answers will come

Seeing the dead girl lying next to the figure of Christ, the Reverend Vanneman takes fright and runs out in pursuit of Howard.

Howard wanders out of the church. The white horse appears from nowhere and walks beside him. Howard has the distinct impression that it has been waiting for him. He jumps on its back and rides toward the mountain.

Howard had never reflected on his experiences with wild white horses in Iran. He has forgotten that he saw a horse like this one on his first day in this country. A white horse always turned up every time he needed help - he was dimly aware of the fact.

The Reverend Vanneman runs out of the church in time to see Howard disappear toward the mountain. He is alarmed. Could Howard have killed the girl? He hastens to Mr. Wilson's house. In her night clothes, Helen opens the door sleepily. The Reverend Vanneman tells her hurriedly about the state in which he had found Howard and about the dead girl. Helen hurries off to get dressed.

Mr. Wilson, having come down and been given the facts, goes with the Reverend Vanneman to the church. Then, Mr. Wright, the schoolteacher, turns up. The news spreads through the compound, and more people arrive at the church. Helen comes in, looks at the dead girl, and leaves in a hurry.

Meanwhile the white horse flies up the side of the mountain, reaching the top with great speed. It stops in the same place where Howard had had his experience on that night.

Howard looks around for the cave but sees only an area that looks somewhat disfigured. He walks up and touches the rock; it is extremely hot. He walks around, touching other rocks, and notices they all feel the way they normally would. Then a breeze hits his face once again, and he gets a bit scared.

Howard realizes that he cannot find the answers he seeks; perhaps they would find him.

He wanders back down the side of the mountain and into the wheatfield. He makes his way to the middle of the field and closes his eyes just to see if anything would happen. Suddenly, he hears Helen's voice. She is calling his name repeatedly. He opens his eyes to find himself in the same spot. Helen is standing next to the carriage, a worried look on her face.

Helen knows Howard is going through something that he cannot explain. The minister had warned her about the lost spirits that roam the mountains.

Howard looks around, and then asks, "What day is it?"

She is startled, but says, "Monday. It is Monday, Howard."

Howard sees Hajji Agha, Hussein Khan, and a few other students of his approaching in the distance.

Howard walks up to them. They all regard him wonderingly. Howard asks, "Where is my horse?"

Helen gets into the carriage and drives up to Howard.

"There are many lost souls around here. What if some kind of devil got into you and is controlling your actions?"

Howard says, "I don't know who is doing what to me. I only know there is some power bigger than myself controlling my fate ... I have no way out. I have to follow my fate. Otherwise I would do injustice to my soul."

He goes up to Helen and grasps her hand. "I know that I love you more than anything . . . but if I must choose . . . between my own love, my life of comfort and ease, and these poor, hungry, suffering people, I must choose them. If I am still alive after we have gained justice, there will be enough time for us to live happily. If I do not make it through, then please forgive me. I cannot live the rest of my life feeling guilty for abandoning these people."

Deep in her heart, Helen understand. But now she says, "I will help you to get out of this. Please let me help you."

"Helen, I know that I will probably die here. I don't want you to suffer because of me. I want you to be free - free and happy. Please understand that the Howard you love is gone now. Set me free. Please let me go in peace with your blessing."

"How can I let you go and watch you kill yourself? You are my husband!"

"I am married to a cause. I set you free and you must set me free."

Howard tries to take his ring off his finger. He realizes that the ring is missing. He looks confusedly at Helen. He sees his horse now standing beside Hussein Khan, who brings over the horse and hands the reins to Howard.

He mounts his horse and rides away. The others follow. Hajji Agha trails behind. He watches the tears run down Helen's face. Then he touches his spurs to his horse's sides and joins the rest of the men up ahead.

Helen stands alone for a while. A soft breeze flows over her. She knows in her heart that she will not see Howard again. He did not belong to her anymore, maybe he never did, but she knows that she must try to protect him. What if she could do something to protect him from being killed? She would live with the guilt for the rest of her life unless she did something.

* * *

The Memorial School carriage is taking Helen and her father to Sardar's house. There is a big crowd outside the house. Sardar's guards approach and escort them inside.

The crowd outside makes a powerful impression on Helen. She sees hunger and despair and exhaustion on all the faces before her. One woman appeared to be carrying a dead child in her arms. Most of them could barely stand.

Something moves decisively within her.

She finds herself at the church and falls on her knees in front of the Christ, weeping. "Oh, my God, I've been such a fool. How arrogant can I be to expect a man to hold two separate loves in his heart? Now I understand how deeply these people live in Howard's soul. Please forgive me, God. If I do not let him go free, then I am in the way of his destiny and the future of our people. I cannot allow him to be imprisoned within his own conscience. I pray to you that you give me the strength to let my love go to do your work. I pray that his soul will live under your guidance. Please give me the strength to be without him. You need him more than I. He belongs to them."

Helen is broken away from her thought by Sardar. He knows why Helen has come. He says, "Mrs. Helen, I will talk to Howard. He should honor his family duty. That should not be questioned. I can fulfill that easily. But how can I fulfill my duty to the people? They want food. They want medicine. And I have no answer or solution for them."

Helen turns to her father. "Father, please ask Sardar to promise me that he will support Howard's cause and fulfill his wishes. Ask him to promise to take Howard under his wing and to let him attack first as he wishes."

Sardar watches as tears form in Mr. Wilson's eyes. Mr. Wilson walks up to Helen and embraces her. He turns to Sardar and explains that she has had a change of heart. Sardar says that he would honor her wishes but has to discuss it with the National Council. From then on Helen begins to help Howard's cause and spends her time helping the people.

* * *

It is Sunday morning, and the church is full. The only empty seat is Howard's, next to Helen. A single carnation has been placed on his chair to remind her of her lost love. Howard has been the subject of controversy among the Americans since his arrival. Many still resent his decision to join the revolution.

But for some, Howard is a part of them now more than ever. The music is loud, and the choir's singing can be heard outside the church. Howard is on the minds of many in the assembly. Doty, the American consul, and Wright, the schoolteacher, sit in the front row, nervously looking at each other. They have both been in constant disagreement with Howard. Doty wants him to return to the school immediately.

Mr. Wright asks The Reverend Vanneman for permission to address the church. Not knowing the subject Mr. Wright has in mind, he allows him to speak.

Mr. Wright begins by saying that Howard has done nothing but cause trouble since his arrival. His teaching methods were unorthodox and he had no respect for his home. He had put the lives of missionaries at risk. He would not obey the laws of the land. This despite the urging of Mr. Doty, who had pointed out to him repeatedly that his behavior was inappropriate.

Mr. Wright's remarks are not received as enthusiastically as he had expected. Some Parishioners look confused, and others just stare blankly. But he is not deterred. He points to Mr. Wilson and the Reverend Vanneman and says, "I am here to ask Mr. Wilson and the Reverend Vanneman to not receive Mr. Baskerville at the school, their homes, or at the church. We must disassociate ourselves from him. This is for the good of the church, the school, the mission, and the American people."

A silence falls through the church. Helen has entered the church holding a child in each arm. Behind her are other women and men holding their starving children. Helen walks to the front.

"Mr. Wright," she says, "some of us choose to fight for this." She points to the starving people now filling the church. She goes on: "And some of us just talk about believing in God or being Christian. If some of us do not have the courage to risk our lives to fight for the truth, we may still have the courage to understand that we have no right to interfere with another man's choices. Howard is free to choose his own path, especially if he is fighting for truth, the right to have a free spirit engulfed in justice and love. With all due respect for your association with the school, it is not your place to interfere in our family affairs or in the church's. This is the house of God, not a place to spread your disdain for a man you barely know. This is not my church or your church. This is the people's church. And although you would wish otherwise, Howard is welcome in this church, our home, and at the school whenever he feels obliged to. . ."

Helen is interrupted by a disturbance at the door that has drawn everyone's attention.

Howard is standing in the doorway with Hussein Khan and Hajji Agha. They are all tired and dusty but have peaceful looks upon their faces. The whole church is silent as Mr. Wilson rises to welcome them. The Reverend Vanneman tells the choir to start the music as Howard begins to walk down the aisle. He walks toward Helen. He is cheered by the gathering; people reach out to shake his hand, but Howard never takes his eyes off Helen.

He knows he is welcome by her side no matter what he might do. He wants to ask for their forgiveness and their blessing for the path he has chosen. He wants to shout out to them that just when you thought you couldn't ask for more, your life changes dramatically; what was important still exists but cannot settle the oceans of your soul. He wants to tell his love that he was sorry and that he had caused trouble without intending to. He does not want Helen or anyone else to suffer, so he would disassociate himself from the school and the church.

He makes sure they know he is a Christian and that he loves his country as much as he now loves Persia and that he is risking his life as he would do in America. With tears in his eyes, Howard looks up and stares at the figure of Christ humbly. He closes his eyes and shouts silently, "Yes, yes, my Christ. I am back to beg you to hear my cries. I am back to beg you to help me and others to open our hearts and eyes. To help us accomplish something good before all the people die."

His eyes remain closed as he continues to talk to Christ. "I am sure that you, my beloved Christ, know peace within your heart is not achieved without freedom. And freedom will not be achieved without sacrifices. Maybe my blood will bring courage and an awakening to the people of Persia. Please help me, my beloved Christ."

When he opens his eyes, he finds himself holding hands with Helen and others through out the church, singing with the choir. This is the last time that the full church would see Howard.

Howard places a kiss on Helen's cheek, rises slowly and walks out of the church. Helen watches him leave, tears running down her face. The whole church is silent; everyone is sad but proud of Howard. The consul turns and looks at the Reverend. Vanneman, Mr. Wilson, and then at the schoolteacher, Mr. Wright. A false smile appears on his face. It seems to say, "If we can't change his mind, we can at least pretend we don't know what he is doing. Perhaps it would be better for all."

Howard now has the full support of the church. Helen misses him terribly. Everyone in the church is praying for Howard's safe return. It is even being said that Mr. Doty was beginning to have a change of heart.

* * *

The shah has gathered all the men he can and sent them to Tabriz. The Russian Colonel Palkoneek Lykhaof has been told to lead the shah's forces into battle. The shah had lost faith in his own officers.

Meanwhile, some of the brigands have deserted the shah and are carrying out looting campaigns on their own. They plunder indiscriminately, sometimes attacking even forces loyal to the shah.

Russian Colonel Palkoneek Lykhaof

* * *

The setting sun illuminates the fort where Howard's men await their leader impatiently.

At last, his figure is spotted in the distance.

Howard gets off his horse. He regards them all fondly.

"We have," he says, at last, "the honor of beginning the attack at Gharamelk!"

There is a lot of cheering. It lasts for a while, then subsides, and finally ceases.

Howard tells them, "Go say goodbye. Go say goodbye to your families and loved ones. Go say goodbye to your memories and to your homes just in case the worst happens. I know that is a frightening thought. But the sooner you face it, the easier the next few days will be. Your mind will be cleared of doubt and fear. I will see everyone tomorrow; we will meet at the school at midnight. Do not tell anyone where we are meeting; it must remain a secret among ourselves and Sardar. God bless you all."

Then he rides away. And the boys scatter slowly in their different directions.

Howard visits Mr. Sharifzadeh's grave. As always, he lays fresh flowers at the site.

* * *

Hajji Agha sits in the corner of his room, scribbling a message. He doesn't know what to write. "Please forgive me, my dear mother. I am who I am. I did this for you and my father. I did it for my sister and brother. I am doing it for my neighbors, the city, and for our country. When I close my eyes, my heart aches. I love you all."

He stops, not knowing what else to write, and seals it in an envelope. He places the letter underneath a jar but quickly retrieves it and sticks it into his pocket as he walks out of the room. He meets his father as he enters the house and quickly runs to the bathroom. His father can tell something is wrong and pretends to be busy. Hajji Agha comes out and walks up to his father nervously. He knows that his father always sees through his deceptions.

He says hurriedly, "I am spending the night with my friends Beerang and Tojjar. We need to study our physics and chemistry; it is becoming more difficult, and we do not want to fall behind. I will see you later. I love you."

Hajji Agha's father watches his son grab some books and head out the door, lost in thought.

Hussein Khan is worried that he will not see many of his friends. He reaches a corner and looks around; he was supposed to meet some of them here, so he waits. His mother does not escape his thoughts and he prays for her silently.

A friend shows up. They wait a little longer, hoping more will show, but move on quickly, knowing they can't wait longer. They go by a friend's house and whistle for him to come out. But they get no response and all the lights in the house go out.

* * *

Hajji Agha sits with Tojjar in his living room in front of a platter of food. Beerang enters. They are unable to eat as they look at the food and think of the starving city.

Tojjar's father looks at the boys with pride in his eyes. He wants to see Tojjar become rich and successful. The boys know it is time to leave. They all get to their feet. Tojjar's father rises with them. He slaps his son hard and shouts to his helper to lock the doors and guard the boys.

He snatches the books from his son's hands and he paces the room. "Are you boys in a hurry to go to hell? Don't you even think about your poor mothers and sisters if you get killed? You have food, a good life, a happy family, what else could you ask for?"

He walks up to Tojjar. "I want you to hear me clearly! You will leave this house only over my dead body!" Then he orders his helper to put Tojjar in the basement.

Hajji Agha and Beerang quietly attempt to leave the house when a loud, panicky knock is heard at the front door.

A smile, triumphant and bitter, appears on Tojjar's father's face. "Why are you boys in a hurry? To see your fathers at the door, perhaps? I sent someone after them to come get you and take you home now."

It did not take long for Hajji Agha's father to appear in the doorway with Beerang's father. Both men look very worried.

* * *

Hajji Agha and his father are walking down the street in silence. His father pulls him against the wall, keeping him in the darkness and protecting him from any bullets. He is terribly worried for his son even though he understands what he is doing. They reach a fork in the road and stop. Hajji Agha's father considers which way would be safest.

He turns around to see Hajji Agha racing away down the street. It hurts Hajji Agha very much to run like this from his father, whom he loves.

His father chases him for a long time but eventually has to stop. He leans against a dark wall. Then he sits down on the ground and begins to pray to God to keep his beloved son safe and to return him home safely. He shuts his eyes.

A hand reaches down and touches his shoulder lovingly. He opens his eyes to see his son standing in the moonlight. He stands up and embraces his son. He holds Hajji Agha against him tightly. His son senses all the love and the sadness in his father.

Hajji Agha's father knows he cannot stand in his son's way.

"Forgive me, father," Hajji Agha says. "I can't live with shame for the rest of my life thinking I did nothing."

Hajji Agha's father looks at him sadly. He smiles through his tears. Then he gives his son one last hug and watches him disappear down the street.

* * *

Meanwhile, Howard is sitting in the library setting down a record of recent events. He has always done this. He leans back in his chair and glances at Helen's window. Then he gets up and goes into the schoolyard. He is wearing the traditional Persian soldier's uniform that Helen had made for him.

He looks into Helen's window. A dim light is on in her room. From within comes the sound of a piano. It warms his heart.

He stands outside silently, watching her play for a few minutes.

Soon be becomes aware that some of his men have come into the schoolyard. He leaves the window and goes to meet them.

* * *

They wait in the schoolyard. Every face shows the tension of the hour. So far, only forty men have turned up. But they cannot wait any longer. Howard tells Hussein Khan to get the men ready.

He, too, is worried. Before they march off, he takes a last look at the window of Mr. Sharifzadeh's classroom.

Fear and doubt leave Howard. His eyes meet Hajji Agha's.

Hajji Agha whispers, "There are too few of us. Shall we wait for a little while longer?"

Howard seems not to have heard. He hugs all his men in turn. "If there are seven of us, we are still a rescue team. Freedom is the greatest achievement of all and the greatest cause that men have fought fo throughout history. After all, what is left for a man to live with when you take his dignity and identity away from him? If we die, we die with honor. My friends, if we live, we will live with dignity and honor. There's no value that can be put on freedom. You are all now freedom fighters!"

He tells them to say goodbye to their school. He wants them to smell the walls, the doors, the blackboard, the essence of the school. He wants them all to recall that their fight started here and now it was time to say goodbye to the past and welcome the future.

The boys walk through the school, quietly at first; then they begin to talk and laugh as their memories return.

Hajji Agha and Hussein Khan sit in their old seats, then get up and walk around the room. Hussein Khan runs his fingers over the chalkboard. He breathes in the scent of chalk. Then he picks up a small piece of broken chalk and puts it in to his pocket.

One of the students walks out of the restroom adjusting his pants. It was pantomime; he hadn't used the toilet. But he was remembering how he had always run out of the toilet, buttoning up his trousers, late for class.

Several other students are in the library looking through books. One boy tears a page out of his favorite book.

Howard walks into Mr. Sharifzadeh's classroom and stares at his friend's picture on the wall. He takes it out of the frame and puts it in his pocket.

Other students enter the room. One takes an eraser and puts it in to his pocket, a memory of Mr. Sharifzadeh.

Hajji Agha walks to the door and stops, afraid to walk out the door. He kneels down and kisses the floor.

Soon, Howard is standing alone in the dark hall holding a candle. He walks out slowly, listening to the echo of his every footstep.

Howard enters the schoolyard. He sees Mr. Wilson leaning on an old rifle and holding an oil lantern. He is wearing a long black overcoat that Howard has never seen.

Mr. Wilson says, tears welling up in his eyes, "My brave students . . . students of the Memorial School . . . I see all of you have become men . . . I can see you are about to start a new chapter in the history of Tabriz . . . the history of Persia. I am honored to be your principal. The Memorial School will not forget such an event. Indeed, someday they will build a memorial here for your brave actions. This is no doubt the greatest and proudest moment I have ever witnessed or been a part of. I am here to present this rifle, which was given to my grandfather by George Washington for his bravery in the American Revolution. He gave it to my father and my late father had passed it on to me, and now I give it to your leader and my son-in-law, Howard Baskerville."

Howard is deeply touched.

Mr. Wilson puts the rifle on Howard's shoulder and embraces him.

But it is getting late, and Howard knows he must get his men going. He says goodbye and they make their way down the streets, listening to the wind play in the trees.

Several men materialize out of the darkness. They are freedom fighters equipped with guns, who want to join them. Howard nods; they need as many men as possible.

They soon reach the street that leads to the mosque, their meeting place. Then Howard leads his men out of the mosque.

It is filled with other groups of fighting men.

Howard and his men gathered before the final attack

Loud cheering announces Sardar′s arrival. Sardar gathers his leaders and begins to go over the details. He summons Howard to his side and talks to him as a father would. He wants to be sure that Howard will come out of this unharmed. He wants to make sure that Howard is careful.

Sardar knows Howard is indifferent to his personal safety. This is what worries Sardar most. They hug and give each other the customary kisses on the cheek and wish each other luck. Howard catches a glimpse of Moore standing in a corner.

As Howard leads his men out of the mosque, Moore approaches him. He tells Howard that he strongly opposes Sardar's decision to attack just then. He suggests that Sardar is behaving irrationally, like a man not entirely in control of his faculties.

He says that Sardar has not been candid with his men. He claims to know that Sardar has been negotiating with the Russians and English who have promised to let supplies of food come through. Why, then, was Sardar still fighting?

Howard stares incredulously at the man.

Moore wants Howard to stop fighting. He says that he, for one, is not going to lead his team into battle.

But he soon realizes that Howard is not to be persuaded.

Howard finally gives vent to his growing irritation. "Dying for justice, truth, and liberty," he says, "is an honor, especially if it is for your land."

His words enrage Moore. He reminds Howard that his land is America, not Iran.

Howard gives him a look of contempt. "My name," he tells Moore, before turning his back on him, "is Persia!"

Howard and his men head off into the woods. They walk past broken-down walls. Fallen trees lie strewn about. They crush fresh-blossomed flowers and weeds underfoot.

The sound of Helen's piano accompanies them.

Howard's nostrils absorb the scent of spring flowers and pine.

These apparently free-spirited men are marching to battle, ready to die in the cause of freedom. Fear and doubt are on everyone's face. Hussein Khan, alone, seems serenely confident.

They arrive at their foxholes, assume their positions, and gaze at the enemy line across the wheat field. Then they settle down to wait for Sardar to give the order.

Bobbing heads are visible through the tall wheat on the enemy's side. Men swing braziers in the air to ignite the charcoal within: preparations for morning tea. Many among them are, no doubt, still asleep.

Howard is aware that his men are tense. Many of them won't catch his eye. One thought is uppermost in their minds: They are heavily outnumbered, only forty of them to the enemy's much greater numbers.

Howard depends on Hussein Khan's bravery and leadership. He has to lead the men in battle. Howard is doubly certain of that now.

The men watch anxiously as Howard disappears behind the trees and the demolished wall. He has gone to survey the enemy's position; to do this he has to get close to their line.

Soon Howard is hiding in the bushes, surveying the enemy line. There are thousands of them and they are ranged against only a few of his men.

But that doesn't daunt Howard for an instant. He is determined to attack and open the road. Food has to reach the starving city.

* * *

They reach the battlefront. Howard goes away to reconnoiter. When he returns, he speaks to his men:

"You are about to enter the battle of your life. I know some of you are scared. I am too. But if we die, we die with honor. If we live, we live with liberty and honor. Life is so painful when you live in fear. But I know after death, we live on. You must not become scared now; you are the same men who were full of passion in training and, just a few minutes ago, ready to fight. Remember who you are and it will be all right."

Under the moonlight, his men watch the tears run down Howard's cheeks.

"You know," he goes on, "life is something strange. Right when you think you are the happiest man, something can happen and change it to your saddest time. You love someone today, you lose them tomorrow. I miss my mother, my sister. I miss Helen."

* * *

Howard sees Mr. Sharifzadeh, in a long, loose white greenish outfit, standing opposite him.

"Don't you understand the answer is not in killing?" Mr. Sharifzadeh says. "It is in love. You just have to open up your heart to feel it. Look, see it for yourself."

Howard opens his eyes suddenly and sees his men staring at him. Among them is the blind, chubby-faced drummer boy. He is playing his drum. Howard realizes that the drummer boy is visible to him alone.

Then he sees an object out in the field of wheat. It is a figure of Christ on a cross.

Howard turns to the drummer boy who is playing more loudly now. Then, just as suddenly, he is no longer there. The boy has been transformed into the sign bearing the name of God that Howard been shown by the two angels. It is the letter that spells the name of God. The Persian artwork revealed to Howard by the green and blue angels fades into view.

Howard watches as the symbol rotates 180 degrees upside down. He sees that the long "y" that had puzzled him before is actually the English letter "L" for "Love."

He looks more closely and discovers that the sign reads "Love" in several languages. He is surprised that he can read and understand them all.

The sound of the boy's drum becomes deafeningly loud.

Mr. Sharifzadeh is walking away through the wheat field. He turns and smiles at Howard and walks on.

The Christ on the cross is now dazzlingly bright. Beams of light are shooting out of it; one is aimed right at Howard.

But Howard finally arrives at what he was searching for all along. The answer comes to him, but too late. He realizes the answer is not in teaching or learning how to kill and destroy. It is in teaching and learning how to love and build. But how can he tell his fighting men this? The men that all along he led the wrong way, teaching them to kill. How can he destroy their passion, their beliefs? What if he were wrong again? Perhaps it is better that he leave them alone to learn for themselves as he did.

Howard rises, his eyes closed, and walks out into the wheat field. His men watch, dumbfounded. Too late to be stopped now, he is walking directly into the enemy's line of fire.

Howard knows that he is walking toward his destiny. He asks God for help. Howard knows that God is trying to send him a message, but he does not yet know what it is.

Howard's thought takes him back home in Nebraska with his family. He walks through the wheat field, brushing the tops with his fingers. His sisters follow, copying his movements. They approach their house where their mother is waiting outside for them.

Howard's heart begins to speak to her. "Dear mother, these days I can feel the footsteps of death creeping behind me. They are relentless and steady. The forever-after death is a white sleep, but one I am now ready to embrace . . . I am no longer afraid. Life can not exist without death. They are, forever, one and together intermixed."

A soft breeze plays on Howard's face. The breeze travels

through the Nebraskan wheat field and resonates across the world, finally whistling softly in the distant wheat field in Tabriz.

"I want to leave you with a soft smile and a kiss upon your cheek. But not forever. I will visit you in your dreams and we all will dance in the white light together. Dearest Mother, it is up to the Universe to write the next chapter. Ideally, it will be a happier one ... "

Howard walks through the wheat field, never taking his eyes off the image of Christ. Hajji Agha and Hussein Khan watch as Howard proceeds, his arms raised high in the air, holding his rifle. The sound of a shot from his rifle starts the fighting.

Blood begins to pour from his chest just as his gun goes off. A bullet had traveled straight toward Howard's chest at the same instant his gun had gone off. It struck his heart with incredible force. Howard kneels on the ground, smiling, his eyes fixed on the image of Christ.

For a moment, no one moves. They know he is gone. Then they hear men from the enemy lines yelling, "The American has been shot! The American has been shot!" This seems to reinvigorate the enemy.

Hussein Khan rises and runs toward Howard, followed by Hajji Agha and a few other men, shooting. But the enemy's cannon forces everyone to drop down and take cover behind small mounds of dirt; bullets rain down on them. Smoke fills the air. They are caught in heavy crossfire. But Hussein Khan would not give up. He presses on to retrieve Howard's body.

Meanwhile, Sardar stands on a rooftop, anxious to know how the fighting had started. A rider appears through the fog and rushes up to the building. He shouts that Howard has been shot. Sardar is motionless for a moment; then he rushes out to his horse. He calls out an order that Ali Musio is to change the direction of his attack. Sardar wants the attack to be concentrated on Howard′s side of the battlefield.

Back in the wheat field, Hajji Agha and Hussein Khan wait for the gunfire to abate. Hajji Agha calls out cautiously, "Sir? . . . Mr. Baskerville? Howard?"

Hussein Khan grabs his gun and sets off, darting and shooting as he dodges bullets. Hajji Agha and a few others provide covering fire. He finally reaches the spot where Howard has fallen. Hussein Khan sits motionless beside the body. He stares in disbelief at the body covered in blood and mud. He only faintly hears Hajji Agha's voice calling his name. He does not notice that he has been shot in the side and is bleeding.

* * *

As bullets from both fronts land around Hussein, he sits motionless. Hussein lifts Howard's body and his rifle. He runs back. Bullets rain on him from both sides. Several bullets hit him. He drops.

Then Hussein Khan feels himself being pushed aside. Howard opens his eyes and rises from the ground, unarmed, unbloodied and unsoiled and screams, "It's hot! It's hot!"

A brownish steam emanates from Howard′s entire body. It travels through the air. Mr. Sharifzadeh appears, very young and happy, and grabs Howard by the hand. ″It will be okay. You are being freed. You are being freed, my friend,″ Mr. Sharifzadeh says. Then a mass of black flying creatures begin to attack Howard. But they are beaten away. Howard walks towards a waiting white horse. He mounts the horse and rides through the battlefield, his hands in the air. Mass of bullets traveling around him but none has any effect on Howard.

Howard rides into the garden that he has seen before. It is the same beautiful garden with a profusion of fruit trees and flowers, surrounded by four rivers of blue water running down to the sea. It is the same garden the old man on the rock had helped him see.

He sees Mr. Sharifzadeh up ahead. He is smiling at Howard, welcoming him.

As he begins to walk around the garden with Mr. Sharifzadeh, he glances around and sees Jesus, Muhammad, Abraham, Moses, Zoroaster and Buddha by the river. They walk along the banks peacefully. And Howard feels their welcoming him.

The white horse leaps into the air, neighing loudly. He turns around and gallops full speed back onto the battlefield. Howard watches the horse stop for a moment, then turn and regard him steadily. He raises his hooves in the air. Several bullets strike the mystical creature and drive it to the ground. But every time, the horse gets up and looks around.

The horse glimpses the representatives of many different religions holding rifles, each shooting at it. Howard and Mr. Sharifzadeh look on, appalled.

Hussein Khan watches in confusion. He wonders if he should believe what he has just seen. He finally hears Hajji Agha's voice yelling, "Hussein, Hussein."

With tears in his eyes, Hussein turns to Howard to see he is laying down cover with blood. He lifts up Howard's body and begins to run. He is struck by several bullets in the arms and legs and he falls to the ground atop Howard's body. Blood is pouring from him, and he knows he cannot stay there. He yells to Hajji Agha to give him covering fire. He gets ready to make a run for it.

Then, without a word, these pampered rich young men begin

to fight like tigers. Soon, the entire wheat field is covered with blood, smoke, and bodies. Hussein Khan makes his way to a clump of trees and falls to the ground, still holding onto Howard tightly.

Many of his men gather around Howard's body.

Sardar rides over and dismounts from his horse. He takes off his hat. He salutes them all. His eyes are misty. He walks to Howard's body and lifts it up. He puts it on his horse, takes a few steps back, and salutes.

Howard's men lead his horse away. Then Sardar mounts his horse, and full of rage, heads toward the battle.

* * *

The whole city mourns Howard's death. The Russian and English consuls meet Sardar. They assure him that the shah would let supplies of food through if Sardar were to call his men off. Sardar does this. What he did not know was that if they had continued to fight for a few more hours, they would have defeated all the shah's forces. The warlords' men were running away, and the Russians were retreating because they were losing too many men.

Howard's body is carried to his father-in-law's house and laid on a bed in the bedroom.

Helen brushes the dirt and dried blood off his face. His face is smooth and the features unmarred. The face wears the same smile as when he fell to the ground.

Helen and her family prepare the body for burial. They remove all his clothes and wash the blood off his chest and back. Helen finds the fatal bullet hole and washes the dried blood off.

* * *

It is the next day, and Howard is dressed in his black suit and laid on the bed, looking as noble as anyone had ever seen him. There is a white carnation in his buttonhole. The house is filled with the sound of music. Outside, a large crowd gathers. Soon, the yard is filled with people. Students from the school and Howard's men form a long line. All are carrying flowers. They enter the house, one by one, to pay their last respects.

A merchant enters with his boy and hands Helen a black cloth to cover the coffin. He claims that it had been brought from a holy place. He had intended it for himself when he died. But he wanted to honor Howard and so he had brought it for his coffin. Helen takes the piece of cloth and holds it tightly. She feels very proud of Howard.

The mass of people outside grows quickly, and soon there is a line several blocks long. They have all come to pay homage to their hero.

The sound of prayers, as Howard's body is once again carried outside, can be heard many miles away. Several Memorial School students carry his coffin to the church. Many have still not had a chance to say goodbye, and follow the coffin to the church, ready to follow him all the way to his grave.

The church is filled with candles. Howard's church is left empty except for the single white carnation. Hundreds gather outside the church. The boys sing a song in Turkish: "There is a happy land . . ." Howard's coffin is covered with black cloth and lined with soft white muslin. It could not be more beautiful. The boys and girls place sixteen exquisite floral wreaths upon it, with the almond blossoms beginning to bloom. Helen begins to weep uncontrollably.

The leaders of the freedom fighters, Sardar, Ali Musio, Bagher Khan and others sit in front. The American consul sits on the right; he looks happy and proud of Howard. All the Europeans, the American bishop, the Muslims, and the Americans fill the church and mourn Howard's death.

All of them admired Howard and believe they have lost a great teacher. They are there to let Howard's soul know that they admire his faith in Christ and his presence in Persia.

Some begin to compare him to Christ because he sacrificed his life for the people; others think he should be honored as a great missionary or as a martyr of Persia. Better yet, a martyr for freedom and justice. One teacher recalls a beautiful passage from Carlyle's writings: "Difficulty, obligation, martyrdom, and death are the allurements that act on the hearts of men."

After the ceremony, Howard's body is carried to his grave, accompanied by an enormous crowd. It is an extraordinary sight, this great throng of people walking down the street to the graveyard.

The crowd is led by a stern old man on a splendid horse; he carries a drawn sword. A man holds up a banner bearing Howard's name as a band plays the Persian military salute. The coffin is guarded by sixteen boys who are followed by Sardar, Ali Musio, Bagher Khan, and Mr. Wilson on horses.

Mr. Wilson watches Howard's students carrying the body and all the Americans surrounding it. The line of people is soon over five miles long. Students line the streets holding their guns in the air upside down, a mark of respect.

The casket is set down beside the grave and everyone begins to gather around. Helen watches the crowd of people fill the graveyard. This further evidence of the people's regard for Howard gives her great joy. The Reverend Vanneman says a prayer. Then he turns to the people of Tabriz who are gathered all around. He talks with passion and deep understanding. "People of Tabriz, we have lost our young man for your freedom. I hope that you will not lose your freedom and will prosper and reach greatness."

Mr. Doty, American consul, and Iranian officials attending Howard Baskerville's funeral in Tabriz

The Reverend Vanneman delivers a short oration after reciting a prayer. An Armenian activist says a few words. But the last and best words come from Sardar. Everything came from deep within his heart and soul.

"Oh, you, the people of Tabriz. Oh, you brave spirits that have risen up to claim your freedom. You must remember our young American friend and brother who loved us and our land enough to shed his own blood. We must never forget that he took up his gun for our freedom and died so we can live with dignity. America gave him deep roots, but Iran has given him wings. You must always feel his presence in your heart. You must tell your children and your children's children. Howard is not just a great son of America; he is a great son of Iranian freedom. You must tell your children that the city of Tabriz is honored to keep his memory alive and he will forever live in our hearts."

Tears streak down Sardar's face as he finishes his address. The Reverend Vanneman reads passages from the Bible as Howard's body is lowered into the grave.

Howard's grave is never bare of flowers. Helen replaces the flowers every day. Before her departure from Tabriz and Persia, she leaves twelve fresh white tulips, and a poem, on Howard's grave. The tulips wilted eventually but the poem she left behind never left Helen's heart. It became a song, a beautiful song that became part of her heart.

Let the flowers stare,
In the silence of the light.
Let the flowers sing,
A silent song.
Let the flowers explore,
The innocence of your heart.
Let the flowers reach,
The beauty of your soul.
Let the flowers bring,
A future,
Full of life, hope and love.
This is the first,
The rest to come,
From my heart to forever,
Friend and love.
I would never forget,
Your wonderful smile.

It is in my heart for ever it comes.
Then:
I sometime wonder,
Why the final word,
Always has to be goodbye.

Later, Annie writes to Howard's mother. "The harvest could not come in Tabriz till there was such a grave: 'Except a corn of wheat had to fall onto the ground and die, it abides alone, but if it dies, it bringth forth much fruit."

After Howard's death, the school is never the same. At first, the students do not want to come. Gradually, persuaded by their parents, they begin to trickle back

Howard's death had affected everyone. All kind of art begins to be made in his memory. Many poems are written for him and his heroism.

The hand-woven tapestry made by the women of Tabriz shows the image of Howard Baskerville. This was meant to be sent to Howard's mother in Nebraska as a gift of appreciation, but it never made it to her.

Helen and Hajji Agha meet often to comfort each other. At one meeting, Helen tells Hajji Agha that she is leaving soon for America. She is going to visit Howard's parents in Nebraska and tell them about Howard. They had to be told what Howard's final wishes were and that he wanted to die in Tabriz. By then, they are at the gate of the garden. The two friends look at each other for a long while and then shake hands.

Hajji Agha watches Helen walk toward the waiting carriage. She gets in and does not look back as the carriage drives away. Helen would never forget Hajji Agha or the place she had lived for so long. A few days later, Hajji Agha hears that Helen has left Tabriz.

Every year activists visit Howard's gravesite in Tabriz to show their respect

* * *

Back in New York:

Reza/Hajji Agha finishes his story as tears run down his face.

The conference room is silent.

"My friends," he says, "we all know that behind every great man, there is a powerful woman. Howard could not possibly have accomplished his quest unaided - and that wonderful woman is here, somewhere among you, to hear these words."

He takes a handkerchief out of his pocket and wipes his running tears. He surveys the room. "Ladies and gentlemen, I am honored and proud to introduce Mrs. Helen Wilson. I ask her to come up here and help honor the memory of my hero, my mentor, my friend, Mr. Howard Baskerville."

Everyone looks around the room.

An elegant woman wearing a long, light green dress rises and walks quietly to the door. Just before she leaves the room Hajji Agha catches a glimpse of her.

He runs through the hotel lobby and onto the street. But there is no trace of her. He finds a deserted bench and sits down dejectedly.

A voice nearby says, "Heroes do not need to be praised. They are already giants."

He turns and finds Helen standing with her sister, Susan, Susan's husband, and their two children.

Helen grasps Hajji Agha's hand. "I know Howard's soul is here. He is always with me. I know he is looking over all of us now. He took his place in history and will forever remain a hero. And as he always said, we have to have much love in our hearts; the more love we give, the more we will feel."

Now Hajji Agha realizes that the note-bearers were Susan's children.

Hajji Agha and Helen talk through the night.

After leaving Tabriz, Helen moved to Nebraska and bought a

farm next to the Baskerville's family's farm. She lived there and never remarried. She had come to New York after learning about the conference and was staying with Susan, who lives there with her family.

* * *

Helen was not wrong; the people of Tabriz and Iran would never forget the memory of their beloved freedom son. The women of Tabriz got together and wove a rug with Howard's portrait on it, intended as a gift for his mother. It never reached America. Now it is kept in a museum in Tabriz that honors Howard, Sardar, and the other heroes of their movement.

Howard's name and the names of his men were inscribed on his gun. This, too, was intended for his mother but, like the rug, it is still in the museum. Every year, poets and activists gather at Howard's grave and sing, chant, and pray to his memory. He has never been forgotten, and his grave is visited by tourists all year round.

* * *

Food did reach the starving people of Tabriz. But then the Russians occupied the city and tried to colonize it. They underestimated the resolve of the people of Tabriz. Inspired by the memory of Howard's sacrifice and many other heroes, the people of Tabriz and Iran, led by Sardar and Bagher Khan, rose up against the Russian invaders and the shah. They marched into Tehran and defeated their enemies. Muhammad Shah was ousted and replaced by his son. The Russians left, and the Parliament was reopened. But sadly, later by England's request and influence, Sardar was put under house arrest in Tehran by the same people that he help to take power. He died poor and lonely as all hero's do.

Mr. Wilson returned to the state. In his absence, the Memorial school lost its momentum and was on the verge of being closed down. So he was asked to go back to Tabriz. Upon his return was a huge celebration by the locals. He died a year later and is buried in Oromieh, in Iran, with his wife. Sardar, Mr. Wilson and Howard, may be gone, but the memory of them will stay in the hearts of the Iranian people forever.

Sardar (Sattar Khan) and his men march in Tehran after the victory

THE END

We Are

In prison within our reason, beliefs and laws,
In prison within our madness, hates and lies,
In prison within our past, futures and eyes,
In prison within our cultures, customs and cause.
We are
Passengers of life, lost in time,
Traveling into the passage
Of uncertain life.
Searching for the truth, to become one.
Then we must;
Hold hands together as one,
Yell with one voice in our heart,
Let go of our madness, hates and lies,
Learn to love others as one does one self.
So:
It would guide the one,
To reach within, to feel the light
That one believes is God!
Isn't this what mankind wants and must?

Ata Servati

Persian/Iranian & World Chronology/TimeLine:

BC 5000-4001	Earliest cities arise in Mesopotamia between Tigris and Euphrates rivers in what now is Iraq.
4241	First exactly-dated year in history
3900	Near the city of Kashan in Iran, first city called "Sialk" is built.
3760	First year of Jewish calendar.
1500's	Medes and Persians, two Aryan groups, settle in Persia/Iran. Each establishes its own territory.
1300s	Moses receives the Ten Commandments on Mt. Sinai.
1000's	Persian Prophet Zoroaster introduces concepts of monotheism, duality of good and evil, angels, heaven and hell. (Good deed, Good thought, Good words.)
1000-960	King David succeeded by his son, Solomon.
836	Assyria, a powerful country west of Persia, invades homeland of the Medes; many other Assyrian invasions follow.
700	The Medes form a unified state, Media, and establish their capital at Ecbatana (now Hamedan in Iran).
625	The Medes reach the peak of their power under Cyaxares, (625 to 585 B.C.); after his defeat, Assyria builds an empire that includes parts of what are now Afghanistan,

	Iran, Pakistan and Turkey.
550	Achaemenid Empire founded by Cyrus II, known as Cyrus the Great (600-529 B.C.).
539	Cyrus captures Babylonia and frees the Jews; later he conquers Palestine, Syria and all Asia Minor.
525	Cyrus's son Cambyses adds Egypt to the Achaemenid Empire.
522	Darius I becomes king; Persian Empire pros pers as he builds roads, establishes shipping lines, and introduces gold and silver coins. At its peak in 500 B.C, this vast empire stretches west into what is now Libya, east to what is now Pakistan, and from the Gulf of Oman in the south to the Aral Sea in the north.
331	Alexander the Great conquers the Persian Empire and burns Persepolis, the capital of Persia.
323-141	After Alexander's death, the Seleucid, dynasty, established by one of Alexander's generals, to rules over Asia Minor.
247	Parthia, located in today's northeast Iran, defeats the Seleucid dynasty and rules Persia.
6	Birth of Jesus.
AD 24	Jesus baptized by John, begins ministry.
29	Jesus crucified.
224	Sassanid Empire is established by Ardeshir I in Persia.
260	King Shapur I of Persia turns back

invading legions of Roman Empire.

325	Church of Nativity built in Bethlehem
330	Constantine I the Great, the Roman Empire's first Christian emperor, rebuilds city of Byzantium, which is renamed Constantinople.
360	Scrolls being replaced by books.
380	Christianity becomes official religion of Roman Empire.
394	Theodosius I becomes emperor of East and West, reuniting the Roman Empire.
400	New Testament completed.
570	Birth of Prophet Muhammad in Saudi Arabia.
591	War between Persians and Byzantine Empire.
610	Islam founded by Prophet Muhammad in Saudi Arabia.
614	Persia conquers Damascus and Jerusalem.
616	Persians overrun Egypt.
625	First year of Muslim calendar.
630	Muhammad leads army of 10,000, captures Mecca; he declares principles of Muslim faith.
633	Arabs attack Persia.
634	Omar I conquers Syria and Egypt.

637 Jerusalem conquered by Arabs.

641 Library of Alexandria burned by Arabs; 600,000 scrolls destroyed.

642 Arabs conquer Persia, introducing Islam.

820-1220 Golden age of Persian Islamic scientists and philosophers.

1220 Mongol armies led by Genghis Khan invade Persia.

1402 Timur (Tamerlane) conquers Persia; at time of his death in 1405, his empire extends from the Euphrates in present-day Iraq to the Indus in India.

1501-1722 Persia is united under Shah Ismail I (Safavid dynasty); Shiism becomes state religion.

1587-1629 Reign of Shah Abbas the Great; pinnacle
of the Safavid dynasty in Persia.

1602 War between Persia and Ottoman Empire.

1623 Shah of Persia, Shah Abbas I, conquers Baghdad.

1694 Hussein becomes shah of Persia.

1722 Safavid dynasty ends as Esfahan is captured by Afghans.

1729-1747 Nader Shah expels Afghans and reunites Persia.

1730 Ashraf, shah of Persia, murdered.

1734-1735 Persia and Ottoman Empire at war.

1747-1779	Karim Khan Zand gains control of Persia and refuses to be called shah or king.
1795-1925	Qajar dynasty; Persia reunited once again.
1796	Agha Muhammad Shah seizes Khurasan, makes Tehran capital of Persia.
1813-1828	Russia takes control of Caucasus region (present-day Georgia, Armenia and Azerbaijan).
1813-1828	Gulistan and Turkmanchay treaties with Persia.
1826	Russia declares war on Persia.
1851	Qujar dynasty forced to give up Persia's Asian provinces to Russia and all claims on Afghanistan to Great Britain.
1853-1856	Crimean War; Great Britain and France join to block Russian invasion of declining Ottoman Empire.
1855	Great Britain and Afghanistan join against Persia.
1856	War between Great Britain and Persia.
1896	Nassr-al-Din, shah of Persia, assassinated.
1906	Qajar dynasty once again forced to give up Asian provinces to the Russians and all claims on Afghanistan to the British.
1906	Persia's first parliament, the Majles, established; first Persian constitution signed by Muzaffar al-Din Shah.

1907	Oil discovered in Persia.
1907	Persia is divided between Russians and British. Northern region goes to Russia and southern to Great Britain.
1907	Shah of Persia succeeded by his son, Muhammad Ali Shah.
1907	Howard Conklin Baskerville arrives in Tabriz, center of the Persian constitutional revolution, and joins Sattar Khan's forces.
1909	Muhammad Ali Shah deposed by constitutional revolution led by Sattar Khan. Revolutionary leader Bagher Khan is replaced by his son Sultan Shah, age 12.
1909	Anglo-Persian Oil Company is established.
1912	Tewfik Pasha becomes Grand Vizier of Persia.
1921	Reza Khan carries out coup in Tehran.
1924	Ahmad, shah of Persia, dethroned. Reza Khan made regent.
1925	Pahlavi dynasty is established by Reza Khan Pahlavi, who becomes shah.
1935	Official name of Persia is changed to Iran.
1941	Reza Shah declares Iran's neutrality in World War II. British and Russians invade Iran; Reza Shah forced into exile and is succeeded by his 12-year - old son, Muhammad Reza Pahlavi.
1951	Muhammad Mossadegh becomes prime minster of Iran; under his leadership, parliament nationalizes oil industry, ending British control over Iranian oil.

1953	Shah leaves the country, but CIA-sponsored coup leads to his return; Mossadegh arrested.
1962	White Revolution is launched by Shah Muhammad Reza, resulting in land reforms and the granting of new rights to workers and women.
1967	Mohammad Reza Pahlavi crowns himself king of kings (emperor of Iran. His wife, Farah Diba, becomes empress. This event causes resentment among some people within Iran.
1971	In a lavish and hugely expensive ceremony, the shah celebrates 2,500 years of Persian monarchy. He is seen as increasingly out of touch with both religious leaders and ordinary citizens.
1974	Annual Iranian oil revenues reach $18 billion after Arab oil embargo (in which Iran does not participate). Sudden wealth also accelerates corruption that will lead to downfall of the shah.
1972	President Richard Nixon visits Iran; strong links are established between Iranian and American military forces. Iran builds world's fifth largest army.
1979	Islamic revolution ends Phalavi dynasty; Shah leaves Iran. On January 20 Ayatollah Khomeini returns to Iran after 14 years in exile. He establishes the Islamic Republic of Iran. Darkest time of Iranian history.
1980	Iraq attacks Iran; the war lasts eight years.
1988	Iran and Iraq agree to a cease fire.

CHARACTER DESCRIPTIONS:

Muhammad Sharifzadeh; An Iranian clergyman who teaches at the Presbyterian Mission's Memorial School in Tabriz and becomes Howard's best friend and mentor.

Sardar (Sattar Khan); A leader of the constitutional revolutionary movement In Tabriz. Howard joins his movement (Sardar means national leader).

Bagher Khan; Another revolutionary leader who has troops under his command and fights side by side with Sardar.

Hajji Agha (Reza Zadeh Shafagh); A Memorial School student who becomes Howard's close friend and joins his group of freedom fighters.

Hussein Khan; Another of Howard's students and one of the bravest in Howard's group of fighters.

Tojjar; One of Howard's student-turned-freedom-fighter.

Ali Musio; A brave fighter and right-hand man to Sardar who also becomes a good friend of Howard's.

Shojah Nezam; A rootless and mercenary warlord hired by Russia and the Iranian shah to attack Sardar.

Rahim Kahn; Another warlord in the pay of Russia and the shah.

Jamal; A rich activist who helps the revolutionary movement.

Mirza Muhammad Mojtahed; A clergyman who leads a group working with the Russians and the shah to defeat the freedom movement led by Sardar.

Mir Hashen; Also working on behalf of the Russians the shah to defeat Sardar.